You Also May Enjoy These Novels
by
Theodore Jerome Cohen

*Death by Wall Street**
*House of Cards**
*Lilith**
*Night Shadows**
*Eighth Circle**
*Wheel of Fortune**
Frozen in Time†
Unfinished Business†
End Game†
Cold Blood††
Full Circle
The Hypnotist‡ ‡‡

* A Detective Louis Martelli, NYPD, Mystery/Thriller
† The Antarctic Murders Trilogy
†† The Antarctic Murders Trilogy (all three books)
‡ Young Adult (YA) novel written under the pen name
"Alyssa Devine"
‡‡ Also available in a special paperback edition for readers
with dyslexia

Visit us on the World Wide Web
http://www.theodore-cohen-novels.com
http://www.alyssadevinenovels.com

The Road Less Taken

A Collection of *Unusual* Short Stories
Book 1

Theodore Jerome Cohen

TJC Press

TJC Press
122 Shady Brook Drive
Langhorne, PA 19047-8027 USA
www.theodore-cohen-novels.com
© *Theodore Jerome Cohen, 2016 • All rights reserved*

The short stories in this book are works of fiction, though some were inspired by real events. With regard to the latter, the author is featured predominantly in "Write What You Know," members the author's family can be found in "A Requiem for Solly," and one of the author's former professors is paid homage in "On Making Coffee and Other Scientific Endeavors." As well, we honor several deceased members of the British Antarctic Survey (BAS) in our story "One Man's Journey Home." Other than these exceptions, any resemblance to actual persons, living or dead, events, or locales in the context of the stories presented here is coincidental. All brand names and product names used in this book are trademarks, registered trademarks, or trade names of their respective holders.

First Edition
First Printing, 2016

ISBN-10: 1517161894 (sc)
ISBN-13: 978-1-5171-6189-7 (sc)

Published in the United States of America
Front cover design by the author

Photo Credits
Front cover art: Big Stock Photo
Frontispiece: Big Stock Photo
Photograph of author: Susan Cohen, 2006

eBook created by eBookConversion.com

Printed by CreateSpace, An Amazon.com Company
Available from Amazon.com, CreateSpace.com, and other retail outlets

To Alice

■

Two roads diverged in a wood and I—
I took the one less traveled by,
And that has made all the difference.

Robert Frost
The Road Not Taken

■

Table of Contents

Author's Note

When I was growing up, visitors to our home in Milwaukee, Wisconsin, often surprised my mother by bringing her a Whitman Sampler, an assortment of boxed chocolates. The cashew clusters, cherry cordials, and maple fudge candies were treats to be savored, and indeed, it took every ounce of self-restraint and then some to keep us from eating more than a few pieces at a time. Short stories are like that. Small, bite-sized morsels of literary ecstasy, they're so tasty and easily digested in one sitting that we're often tempted to gobble them up, one after the other, in pursuit of a reading "high."

This collection of short stories is like a Whitman Sampler. What you'll find here are, in some cases, excerpts adapted from some of my novels, as in the case of "Requiem for Solly" or "And Then There Were Two." In another case, the material is based on an idea I used in a Young Adult (YA) novel written under my pen name "Alyssa Devine." The storylines in both cases involve a fortune teller and the use of tarot cards. I'm particularly proud of "Unforgiven," the story of a man who was asked by his dying father to seek out and thank his World War II Army sergeant for the privilege of having served under him at Normandy and in the Battle of the Bulge. Using some insightful suggestions from the editorial board of the literary magazine *CARVE*, I resubmitted the story to *Glimmer Train*, where it won Honorable Mention in that magazine's September, 2015, Family Matters competition. Given that *Glimmer Train* receives between 2,000 and 3,000 submissions a month, I'll take it!

This book is a literary "sampler," to be sure, and one filled with bite-sized morsels sure to please any palate. Many are based on real events, some even from my own life, which leads us to the first story in the book: "Write What You Know."

I hope you'll take your time to savor every word.

Theodore Jerome Cohen
Langhorne, Pennsylvania
January 20, 2016

Acknowledgements

As always, Susan—the love of my life—provided vital suggestions, insightful editing, and most important, unswerving support during the development of the manuscript. I also want to thank Commander William Alden Lee, U.S. Navy (ret.), for the many suggestions he offered, all of which helped to improve the readability of my stories. Thanks, too, to Sharon Diggans, Library Media Specialist, Neshaminy High School, Bucks County, Pennsylvania, who generously volunteered to chase down those ever-elusive typos. The suggestions of Matthew Lampede, Editor-in-Chief, *CARVE* literary magazine, and his reading committee regarding the development of the story "Unforgiven" are gratefully acknowledged. As well, I sincerely appreciate the support and encouragement I received from sisters Susan Burmeister-Brown and Linda B. Swanson-Davies, Founders and Editors, *Glimmer Train* literary magazine. Finally, Bob Mehta and his team at eBookConversion.com, my "go to" conversion house, worked their usual magic and produced the Kindle version of this book in record time.

The Road Less Taken

SUPPOSED CAUSE OF THE CHICAGO FIRE. MRS. O'LEARY AND HER COW.

**Catherine O'Leary and her infamous cow,
October 8, 1871**

Write What You Know

Write what you know . . . arguably the most important lesson in writing I ever learned! It was my mother who taught me this lesson. She did so when I was nine. How it came about is an interesting story. (Well, I think it's interesting or I wouldn't be telling it to you.) But more than that, from an historical perspective, I think you might get a kick out of seeing the first eleven words of what was destined to be an 1100 word "opus."

My story begins in 1871. No, that's not the year of my birth . . . that came a few years later. But if you live in Chicago, have relatives who live in Chicago, or ever traveled to Chicago, you might recognize the year.

Yes, it was on October 8, 1871, that Catherine O'Leary's infamous cow, the one who kicked over a lantern, started a three-day conflagration that reduced the Windy City to ashes. Among other things, the city went "dry," which is to say, there wasn't a drop of beer to be had within 100 miles.

But fear not. Into the breach stepped Joseph Schlitz. Now, this wasn't the first time Mr. Schlitz had taken advantage of a tragedy. A lowly bookkeeper at the August Krug Brewery in the 1850s, he was in the rather fortunate position of being in the right place at the right time when old man Krug departed this earth in 1856. Within a few years, Schlitz changed both Krug's widow's name and the brewery's to his. It was in early October, 1871, then, that the Joseph Schlitz Brewing Company started shipping beer to Chicago like it was going out of style. The result, of course, was, it made Milwaukee—and Schlitz—famous!

So it was that in 1944, just before the end of World War II, the Family Cohen found itself in Milwaukee. By 1947, when I was nine, we were living near 17th and Lloyd Streets on Milwaukee's West Side, where my younger brother and I attended the Lloyd Street

3

Elementary School. The school was located about one-half mile from the house. We left each weekday for classes at exactly "9-9," as we used to say—quarter to nine in the morning—with me responsible for getting my brother to school (and, of course, home again). This was necessitated by the fact my father had already left for work while my mother was busy with my baby sister.

Having to shepherd my brother to and from school didn't leave much time to explore the neighborhood in the morning, so days on which he stayed home for one reason or another were to be coveted. Why? Because on those days, it meant by leaving slightly earlier, I was free, for example, to stop at Pete's Tavern, which was located a block from the house. My intent was always to learn whether or not he had any empty cigar boxes into which I could put my "stuff" . . . baseball cards, marbles, a stray ball and jack, my Duncan Yo-Yo, chalk...whathaveyou! Stuff!

What? You're surprised a nine-year-old could boldly walk into a tavern on his way to school without anyone batting an eye. Hey! This was Milwaukee! And this wasn't the only tavern on my route to school, by the way. Sooner or later I hit them all during the school year.

And when I left Pete's, I'd move on to the back of the slaughterhouse down the street where, after climbing the back stairs, it was possible by peering into the windows to determine whether cattle or sheep were being processed that day.

Frankly, on the days I was alone, it's a wonder I made it to school at all.

But it was after school that the real fun began. By accident one day I found a garage in an alley several blocks from my house that contained a stable with four ponies. Shetland mares all, they were owned by the father of a boy who became a good friend. His name was Stefan. His father used to give children rides on Sundays at local parks on the north and west sides of the city. The ponies fascinated me, and I never passed up an opportunity to sneak over to visit them and Stefan after school before running home to practice the piano.

Occasionally, when no one else was around, Stefan would let me sit on one of the gentler ones, easily distinguished from the others by her shiny black coat and a white star under her forelock.

4

"Come on, Stefan, let's play some stickball in the alley before I have to go home," I'd often call after school when I got within earshot of the little stable.

"Can't, Teddy," was Stefan's forlorn reply more often than not. "Must do stable." Stefan did not speak English well. His family, like several others in his neighborhood, had immigrated to the United States from Eastern Europe following World War II with the help of the Roman Catholic Church. Still, he and his little sister, Kasienka, were the only two in their family who spoke much English, and only then because of having attended public school. His father, a janitor, worked at two jobs during the week while his mother cleaned houses for women on Milwaukee's East Side. Stefan and Kasienka attended Brown Street Grade School, so at least during the day, their parents did not have to worry about them. But after school, it was Stefan's job to muck out the stable as soon as he got home.

The alley behind our house was quite interesting as well. Among other attractions was a man who garaged his midget racer several garages to the north of where my father stored his Packard.

And not that much farther up the alley was where Old Ned, the ragman's horse, was stabled. Remember, the war had only ended two years earlier . . . the American truck and automobile industries were still getting back on their feet. In Milwaukee, horses still were used to help deliver milk, pull trash and garbage wagons, pull snow plows, and even deliver ice. (Yes, not everyone had an electric refrigerator in 1947.) But back to my writing lesson and to the incident that triggered my first introduction to prose, as it were. Enter "Jimmy," the rat terrier.

Jimmy and his partner, another, smaller rat terrier, used to come down our alley almost every evening just after the sun set with their owner, a grizzled old man with at least five-days stubble on his face. Carrying a long stick, he would poke around the garbage cans in the alley, the intent being to scare rats into the open for Jimmy and his partner to dispatch. For me it was great sport just to walk with them. And so, whenever possible, while my father was at work and my mother was busy with my younger brother and sister, I snuck out to walk the alley with Jimmy & Company.

Until one night I got caught. And therein lies the tale . . . my first English assignment from my mother, a 1100-word tome comprising the following sentence written one-hundred times:

5

I will not walk in the alley with the rag man.

It demonstrated, quite painfully, that writing about the things you know is *very* important. It's a lesson I never forgot and something you might want to keep in mind as you ponder your Great American Novel.

———————————

The illustration above, from *Harpers*, 1871, depicting Mrs. O'Leary with her cow, is in the public domain (Source: Wikimedia Commons).

An illustrated version of this story can be found on the author's blog:

https://www.goodreads.com/author/show/3251724.Theodore_Jerome_Cohen/blog

The author's father, Solly, holding the author in 1941, well before the violin ever was a part of their lives together.

Requiem for Solly

"**So,** have you thought about what you want to be when you grow up?" she asked, gently prodding her husband of 41 years.

They were sitting on a park bench near Triton Fountain in Queen Mary's Gardens, The Regent's Park, breathing in the early morning air and delighting in the awakening of the spring flora. The two had been in London for the week, staying at The Langham, their favorite hotel. Now, only a day remained before their scheduled departure for Philadelphia.

He turned and smiled. *She does have a way of getting to the point,* he thought. "It's not that I haven't been thinking about it. But after running like hell for the last 39 years, it's a little difficult figuring out what to do next."

The breeze picked up, and he watched as she brushed a stray hair from her forehead. Her emerald green eyes sparkled, the same as they did the day they first met at the University of Wisconsin in Madison decades earlier, when he was a grad student in physics and she, a freshman . . . the day he fell in love with her at first sight.

Truth be told, he had given a lot of thought to what he might do now that he was about to retire. The possibilities were endless. Start his own business? Purchase a going concern? Donate time to one or more charities?

Identifying possibilities wasn't the problem. But everything that came to mind lacked one thing, and he couldn't quite put his finger on it. Missing was something personal, something deeply emotional, something that would require him to reach deep within himself and fulfill some vision. For whatever reason, whatever it was that was missing simply would not come into focus.

He had gotten only the slightest glimmer of this vision a few days earlier when, after his wife left their hotel room to go shopping

9

at Oxford Circus, he sat alone and watched a performance of Shostakovich's *Symphony No. 6* on BBC Television. Played by the London Symphony Orchestra, the images of the musicians held him spellbound. In particular, he could not take his eyes off the concertmaster. He marveled at the maestro's mastery of the violin.

He, too, had once played the violin, played it well, in fact, having started lessons in 1948 at the age of nine. His teacher, a German immigrant, helped him to achieve remarkable results within a very short period of time. Recognizing the boy's talent, his father, Solly, hired a more professional—and demanding—teacher, a graduate of The Juilliard School. As well, Solly replaced his son's relatively inexpensive turn-of-the-century fiddle made in Markneukirchen, Germany, with a mid-eighteenth-century Italian instrument characterized by its stunning bear-claw spruce table and one-piece flamed maple back. Solly, a self-made industrialist, knew the value of good "instruments."

"If you're serious about your work, then you need good tools!" Solly was often heard to say, whether at home or in his manufacturing facility on Milwaukee's South Side.

Under the direction of his new teacher, the young violin student made huge strides in technique and virtuosity. Daily practice—at least two hours a day, every day, including weekends—consisted of 30 minutes of scales followed by work on the composition of choice. Included were the big "warhorse" concertos of Brahms, Tchaikovsky, Bruch, and Beethoven as well as the celebrated works of Sibelius, Dvořák, and Goldmark, among others. Each piece, in turn, was mastered before turning to the next.

Not content to merely provide his son with lessons, Solly also made time for them to attend performances of famous violinists in Milwaukee and Chicago.

"What are you smiling about?" his wife asked as they rose to walk back to The Langham.

"Oh, nothing," he said, waving off her question. "I was just thinking about the time my father took me to Chicago in 1953— when I was a freshman in high school—to hear Isaac Stern perform Brahms's *Violin Concerto in D major*."

"That must have made quite an impression on you."

He nodded, stroking his chin. *Of course it had made an impression! How could it not have?* "Oh, yes. There he was, standing just feet from where we were sitting, one of the greatest violinists of all time."

That wasn't the only such performance his dad had arranged for them to see. Among others, they also had attended performances of Ruth Tengwall playing Wolfgang Amadeus Mozart's *Violin Concerto No. 5* and Arthur Grumiaux playing the Bartók *Concerto No. 2 for Violin and Orchestra*. He knew all the while what his father was thinking: *I want my son to become a concert violinist.* That was the old man's dream. That was what he lived for.

Solly loved music—operas were his favorite form of entertainment. But as the fourth child in a family of seven children growing up in an immigrant household in the early 1900s, he was given few opportunities and music lessons were not among them. After graduating from a local technical school, he found work in the shipbuilding industry on Lake Michigan north of Milwaukee. This left precious little time even for listening to the operas in his extensive 78rpm record collection. Still, he was determined to expose his children to the world of music. And when his eldest son demonstrated virtuosic skills using the violin, Solly was convinced he should become a concert violinist. They never spoke about it, of course. Sometimes the potential for conflict between a father and son causes things like this to go unspoken.

Indeed, in this case, the potential for conflict was real. An early introduction to electronics so captured the son's imagination that if he wasn't in school or practicing the violin, he was reading communications magazines or building radios and other small electronic devices. Solly took notice of these "distractions," as he called them, but they only steeled his resolve to convince his son that his future lay in the field of classical music, not in the more mundane fields of communications or electronics.

"Yes," he said, as they continued walking up Regent Street toward The Langham, "seeing Stern and the other violinists of the day was thrilling. But I knew why my father took me to these performances."

"Why was that?"

"Because even though we never discussed it, I knew he wanted me to become a concert violinist. To tell him then that I wanted to pursue a career in engineering would have made him angry. And frankly, being the dutiful firstborn, always wanting to please, I couldn't even bear the thought of disappointing my father—at least not at that point."

"So, what did you do?" she asked, putting up an umbrella to shield them from a spring shower that had suddenly overtaken them.

"Pretty much continued to let events unfold by themselves. I already was concertmaster of my high school orchestra. Thank God that didn't take much effort. But what really threw me for a loop was when my orchestra teacher asked me to try out for the Milwaukee All-City Senior Orchestra. Now there were two people I couldn't let down . . . my teacher and my father."

"So—?"

"So, my teacher and I selected the *Sarabande con Variazioni* by Johan Halvorsen as the piece I would play at my audition. It has six sections. I was certain the person conducting auditions would only want to hear a portion of one section, but which one? All I could do was learn the entire piece."

"And—?"

"Are you always this talkative?"

She laughed, grabbed his arm, and hugged him.

"Well, the man conducting the auditions—I think his name was Shekoski—led me into a small practice room, had me play some rather difficult scales reaching into the seventh position, and then asked me to take out my sheet music. After placing it on the stand, he opened it to the first page, raised his eyebrows, turned and looked at me for a second or two, and then told me to begin at the top. So, I'm thinking, 'Okay, I'll work down the first page and then, after a few lines, he'll probably ask me to stop.' After all, he had a lot of people waiting and really couldn't spend a lot of time with any one person."

She nodded. "And—?"

"And I started playing. I have to tell you, I was surprised by the 'brightness' of my instrument's sound. Meanwhile, Shekoski is scribbling away in his little notebook like it's going out of style. After a few minutes, he laid the book aside, leaned his head back, closed his eyes, and just sat there, listening to the music. When I'd finished playing the first section—the entire *andante lento*—Shekoski didn't move for several seconds. His eyes were still closed, and he seemed to be deep in thought. Then, he took a deep breath, slowly opened his eyes, took up his pen and notebook, and scribbled something next to my name. The next thing I knew, he stood, put out his hand, shook mine, and told me to have a nice evening."

"That's it? 'Have a nice evening.'? Not a word about how you played, whether or not he liked the piece you performed? Just 'have a nice evening'?"

"Yep! That was it! Don't let the door hit you on the way out!"

"I didn't know what to make of it. So now I'm having major doubts about myself and my playing. Should I have selected something less difficult? Did my double-stops—you know, playing two notes simultaneously—need more work? I'm thinking of every possible mistake I might have made."

She nodded again, sympathizing with him.

"And meanwhile," he continued, "I'm walking back to where my father is waiting to drive me home. Man, talk about giving someone the 'third degree.' My dad had so many questions regarding what happened during the audition I could barely get a word in edgewise. But I finally was able to explain that everything *seemed* to have gone well and how unusual it was for Shekoski to allow me to play the entire first section. When he heard that, my dad was elated."

It stopped raining as they passed the Polish Embassy, and she quickly shook, collapsed, and put her umbrella back in its protective vinyl sheath. "Well, don't keep me in suspense! What happened next?!"

He laughed. "Oh, ye of little patience. Well, long story short, I tied for concertmaster of the All-City Senior Orchestra. Matthew Edgington from West Division High School was selected as the other concertmaster. Let me tell you, he was one talented guy! And for my troubles, based on a suggestion made by Mr. Shekoski, the sponsors of the music festival invited me to play the violin part of Mozart's *Sinfonia Concertante for Violin and Viola in E flat major* with full orchestra accompaniment, during the second half of the concert."

"Wow, that was quite an honor."

"Oh, yeah," he deadpanned. "I was thrilled," throwing her one of *those* looks, as if to say, "I certainly didn't need that!"

"Somehow I have a difficult time believing that," she responded. "I'll bet you loved every minute."

"Well, I certainly didn't need the added pressure. And neither did my father. I thought they were going to have to double his heart medication. After he heard about the duet, his blood pressure must have gone through the roof. He insisted on sitting in on every rehearsal and checked in with me at home by telephone every afternoon—twice—to see how practice was going. You knew him. You know how overbearing he could be."

"Oh, yes. I can only imagine. So, what happened at the concert?"

"Well, the first portion of the program went off flawlessly. Matthew, who served as concertmaster here, was at his best, and when the last note of Dvořák's *Symphony No. 9*—the New World Symphony—sounded, the audience burst into applause. Immediately following intermission, Lissa Wilson, a violist from Rufus King High School, joined me in playing the *Sinfonia Concertante.* We had practiced together once a week, an hour before orchestra rehearsal, for more than a month. This was in addition to the work we did at home by ourselves. We felt very confident."

"I'll bet it was exciting to get up in front of all those people."

"It was a thrill, all right. The Milwaukee Auditorium held 10,000 people, if you can believe it, and every seat was filled!

"Anyway, the conductor added to the evening by providing some historical information about the composition, including the fact that Mozart, himself, had written the cadenzas in all three movements. He then told the audience to listen carefully to the final movement, the *presto,* because of the interplay between violin and viola."

"Gosh, I would give anything to have been in the audience. I'll bet you looked handsome."

He chuckled. "This is why I love you so," he said, putting his arm around her, drawing her close, and kissing her on the cheek.

"Anyway, with all in readiness, the conductor's baton poised, we set off, beginning with a long, majestic orchestral introduction. The second movement, of course, is slow, but the third is a spirited romp in which Lissa and I chased each other into the higher reaches of our instruments. Not a sound could be heard from the audience. I swear, it was like everyone was holding their breath. You could have heard a pin drop between movements.

"I have to say, our playing was pure perfection, with its precise intonation and our absolutely perfect synchronization with each other and the orchestra. I'm sure it was everything Solly wanted, no *prayed*, it would be."

"And then what?"

"Well, when the last notes died away, for just the smallest fraction of a second, the auditorium was absolutely silent. Then, all hell broke loose. People literally jumped to their feet and started clapping and whistling. I'd never heard anything like it before. And it seemed to last forever. Every time Lissa and I tried to return to our seats in the orchestra, the applause intensified, causing the conductor to motion us back for another bow. I looked to where my dad was sitting. Tears were streaming down his face. We, of course, gestured our appreciation to the conductor and the orchestra, whereupon the conductor would motion for the entire orchestra to rise and take a bow. Nothing, however, seemed to bring silence to the hall until minutes later, when the audience, exhausted, fell back into their seats."

Turning, she saw him wipe a tear from his cheek. Quickly returning her gaze to the pavement, she took his arm, and they continued walking toward the hotel.

It was several minutes before she spoke again. "Well, you obviously didn't become the concert violinist your father wished you would become. So, how does this movie end?"

"Several weeks later I played in my high school's combined orchestra and band concert, followed by the orchestra's participation in our graduation ceremony—*my* graduation ceremony. There, following the playing of *Pomp and Circumstance March No. 1,* we struck up a medley of songs from the musical *Carousel*, placed our instruments in their cases, and took our assigned seats in the audience. It was June, 1956, and that was the last time I played the violin."

"How did that make you feel?" she asked. "I mean, after all that hard work, how could you just walk away from the violin, especially given how much you loved the instrument."

"The truth is, it was my father who loved the violin. To me, it had become a burden and one I no longer could bear. The hours and hours of practice, combined with attendance at performances in Chicago and Milwaukee, had simply exhausted my love for the instrument. Emotionally, I had nothing more to give."

"Didn't your father attempt to discuss this with you as time went by?"

"Oh, yes. Remember how he used to call after you and I had settled on the East Coast? He encouraged me repeatedly to take up the instrument again but finally gave up in early 1968, a few months

15

before he died. It was the last time we spoke. In the end, my brother told me he commissioned my former teacher to find a buyer for my beautiful Italian violin. The proceeds were donated to charity."

"A dream denied can be a terrible thing," she said, taking his arm as they walked up the stairs into the hotel.

"I'm sure he was devastated," he said, following her into the lobby. "Solly's gone now, but perhaps there's something I can do for him, and for me, when we return home."

"What's that?"

"Turn my life in a new direction by fulfilling the vision he had of me becoming a concert violinist."

Photo by Myrtle B. Cohen, the author's mother.

For the fictionalized story of the author's life as a violinist, read the novel, *Full Circle: A Dream Denied, A Vision Fulfilled.*

http://www.amazon.com/dp/Boo2YNSC88

The author, a future Antarctic explorer, gets a needed assist with his sled from his father, grandmother, and cousin, Fond du Lac, Wisconsin, January, 1940

And Then There Were Two

The three Chilean servicemen in the launch—Chief Warrant Officer Raul Lucero, Chief Petty Officer Eduardo Bellolio, and First Sergeant Leonardo Rodríguez—were on the hunt for seals. Many would be needed for the sleddogs wintering over at Chilean Army Base Bernardo O'Higgins on the North Antarctic Peninsula during the austral winter of 1962. But now it was the 1961-62 austral summer. The three men, ostensively taking a break from the rigors of unloading the Chilean transport ship *Piloto Pardo,* which had brought participants in the XVI Chilean Expedition to the Antarctic, had ventured out among the islands around the base to talk about a division of spoils. More specifically, they had gone out in the launch to talk about the division of the millions of dollars in currency, negotiable securities, coins, and jewelry Lucero and Bellolio had stolen from the *Banco Central de Chile's* branch in Talcahuano—a branch they had been sent to guard—following the magnitude 9.5 Chilean earthquake of May, 1960.

The loot from the bank, improbable as it may seem, had been secreted in a refrigerator purchased by Lucero at a local appliance store in Talcahuano at the time of the robbery. Now the appliance, crated, was stored at Base O'Higgins. At the time of the robbery, Bellolio could not understand why Lucero had purchased the appliance—a new, imported, top-of-the-line, 1960 Hotpoint 18-cubic-foot yellow refrigerator. It barely fit into the small military truck they had commandeered from the Navy motor pool at the dock.

"Why did you do that?" asked Bellolio, scratching his head as he helped Lucero uncrate the appliance and began packing loot into the drawers, shelves, and freezer compartment. "What good is it? Come on, we'll take some of the money, coins, and jewelry, tuck

19

them into our pockets, and continue about our business as if nothing had happened."

That was not good enough for Lucero. "I think I know how we can get everything out of here, Eduardo."

"With a refrigerator?"

Lucero shook his head and gave his subordinate an exasperated look. "Look, my old boyhood friend Leonardo Rodríguez—he's a sergeant in the Army now—is scheduled to rotate into Base O'Higgins with the 16th Expedition to the Antarctic a year from this December. Under military regulations, he can take one or two large appliances with him that were shipped into the country from the United States or Europe for sale in Chile—you know, luxury appliances like refrigerators and stoves. And . . ." He paused to heighten the drama of the moment. "And . . . any appliances he purchases are stored at the base during the summer while he serves in Antarctica.

"So, all we have to do is load up this refrigerator with the currency and other stuff we just took from the safe deposit boxes, repack and reseal the appliance in its original crate—reinforced, for sure—and present it, together with the necessary paperwork, to the Navy Dock Master in Talcahuano. From there, the crate goes to the Fleet Warehouse here before it gets shipped to Punta Arenas for the voyage to Antarctica next year."

Bellolio was all ears.

Lucero continued. "In March of '62, when the Expedition returns to Chile, his appliances get shipped back to his home in Arica without his having to pay import duties on the original purchase. Best of all, the shipping charges, from the dock in Talcahuano to Antarctica, back to Chile, and finally to Arica, will be paid by the Navy. It's a perk, Eduardo—*un incentivo*. It's something offered by the government so military personnel will volunteer for hazardous duty in Antarctica."

"And then—?" asked Bellolio, who still had a bit of quizzical look on his face.

"Come on, Eduardo!" yelled Lucero impatiently. "What the hell's the matter with you? Don't you understand nothin'? Once the Expedition's over and the crated appliance is delivered to Rodríguez's home in Arica, we meet there, uncrate it, take our shares, slip across the Peruvian border, and go our merry ways."

Lucero grinned and threw his hands in the air as if the entire matter were a *fait accompli*.

Bellolio was awestruck! He stood staring at Lucero, his mouth and eyes wide open, acknowledging the beauty and simplicity of the idea. A smile slowly enveloped his entire face. Then, just as slowly, the smile turned to a frown.

"What if Rodríguez won't go along with your plan?"

"You leave that to me. He's always complaining that he never has enough money to provide good things for his wife and family. So, I'll make the refrigerator a gift to him. In addition, I'll offer him cold, hard cash . . . $1 million dollars, U.S. currency. There's more than enough here!

"Actually, he won't have a choice. By the time he finds out what we did, the refrigerator might already be in Antarctica. Who knows?

"Sometimes you just gotta make decisions for people, Eduardo!"

Except things did not work out quite the way Lucero planned. Once on the seal hunt and apprised of the situation in which he had been placed by his boyhood friend, Rodríguez tried to get his head around the number.

"A million bucks, huh? U.S. money?" He could not even comprehend what $1 million looked like. "I don't know, Raul, it's awful risky. I don't want to spend the rest of my life busting rocks."

Rodríguez pondered what he had been told, weighing the risks against the benefits. Some twenty minutes after Lucero had first apprised him of his plan, Rodríguez became agitated. Lucero cut the boat's engine.

"Look, dammit, I'm the one that's taking all the risk here!" stammered Rodríguez. "If someone starts digging into that crate and finds the loot, it's my name that's on the manifest and shipping documents. And I'm not taking the fall for this by myself! You didn't give me a choice in the matter! I'm the one with the family who will have to sit on my share for at least a year until things cool down while you two are off having a great time spending yours in Peru without having to wait. I want $2 million in U.S. dollars. And some gold, too!"

Bellolio's face turned red. "You can't do that!" he shouted.

Out of the corner of his eye, Lucero saw Bellolio reach for his switchblade. Their eyes locked. Lucero's stare convinced Bellolio to take his hand out of his pants pocket.

21

Lucero turned to Rodriquez and put his hands into the air, palms up. "All right, all right, what you say is true, Leonardo.

"Fair is fair. You and I go back a long way, and you're right, we didn't give you a choice. You'll have your $2 million in U.S. currency and 300 gold U.S. $20 coins, too." He held up his left hand to silence Bellolio before the man could say anything.

"Let's go, Eduardo, we're running out of time. We have to bring back at least one seal or people are going to suspect we were out here doing something more than hunting." He started the engine, using the lowest throttle setting to minimize the boat's wake.

The engine was operating at its quietest now, all the better for them to surprise seals that might be resting on icebergs in their path.

Slowly they made their way among the sea ice. The only sounds heard were the low, throaty sound of the engine's exhaust and ice scraping the bow and sides of the launch.

Turning to his right, Rodríguez spotted two forms, both long and gray, laying on a small, flat iceberg. He turned around and gestured wildly to Lucero and Bellolio with his arms to get their attention. Then, motioning with his head, he whispered loudly through cupped hands, "Over there! Over there! Weddell seals."

The seals were lying on a flat, rectangular piece of floating ice about ten feet by fifteen feet in size. Rodríguez immediately signaled Lucero to kill the engine. As the launch slid silently past the iceberg on which the seals lay, they awoke, and one slipped quietly into the water. As the other began moving slowly toward the edge, Bellolio, ever impatient, picked up a rifle, turned quickly to his right, and without taking aim, shot it. Unfortunately, he only wounded the seal. As it lay writhing on the ice, blood spurting from its head wound, Rodríguez berated Bellolio.

"Just like you swabs! The only person safe when you have a rifle in your hands is the person you're shooting at! I guess the best way to put the thing out of its misery and attach a rope to him so we can tow him back to the base is to get on the ice and put a knife through his heart."

Rodríguez motioned for Lucero to restart the engine and for Bellolio to take the boat to the iceberg. Once it touched the ice, Rodríguez jumped over the side with one end of a rope and knelt beside the seal. Preoccupied with killing the animal, he failed to see

Lucero throw the other end of the rope into the water while at the same time directing Bellolio to back the boat away.

By the time Rodríguez had killed the seal and tied the rope around its neck, the launch was more than thirty feet from the iceberg and backing away at a good speed.

Rodríguez was stunned! "What are you doin', Raul? Come back here! We need to drag this seal back to the base."

"I'm sorry, Leonardo," shouted Lucero, "but we can't take any chances. I thought we could make this work, but you had to get greedy. I'm not sure that once we get everything back to your home in Arica, you will be able to keep your mouth shut long enough for us to get to Peru. So, we're going to have to leave you here."

Rodríguez jumped up and down on the ice and screamed. "Bastards! Bastards! You will rot in Hell!"

Small ripples radiated from around the edges of the iceberg, rapidly carrying the sound of Rodríguez's boots hitting the hard surface through the water toward the sensitive ears of any nearby orcas.

Lucero was the first to spot them . . . a pod breached the surface 300 feet to the port side of the launch. He put his index finger into the air and made a circular motion with his hand, at the same time calling to Eduardo. "Turn the boat around . . . slowly. But get us away from here *now!*" Meanwhile, holding the throttle back so as not to attract the orcas' attention, he used his compass to obtain a bearing on Base O'Higgins.

The pod continued moving toward the iceberg on which Rodriquez was standing. He saw them coming, but before he could steady himself, one of the killer whales put his head on the ice, tipping it toward him and using his weight to break off a large piece.

Rodríguez dove for the surface and grabbed the seal, its body covered with blood . . . blood that now was oozing all over the ice and into the water. He took out his hunting knife and plunged it into the ice. This would give him more leverage in the event the orcas attempted to up-end the iceberg.

With the sun shining brilliantly from above, the orca pod, looking up from below, interpreted the shadows they saw as *two* seals lying on the ice.

One by one the orcas placed their heads on the iceberg, attempting to use their massive weight to tip the "seals" into the water. But by holding onto the dead seal, spreading his legs, and

23

holding onto his knife, Rodríguez managed to maintain his position.

Two minutes passed.

Then, to his left, Rodríguez saw a wave coming toward him. This isolated two-foot-high wave could only have been made by living creatures. He had heard stories about how killer whales coordinate their actions to push a wall of water before them in an attempt to upset a small iceberg on which a seal or a penguin has taken refuge. *My God, the orcas are working together to create waves. They are trying to tip the iceberg so that I will be thrown into the water!* The wave passed under the iceberg, but it failed to dislodge either Rodríguez or the seal to which he now was desperately holding tight.

The sea became quiet again. Rodríguez looked to his left, then to his right. *What the hell am I going to do?* He was panic-stricken. "Lucero! You son of a prostitute! I will kill you!"

For an instant he thought about how Lucero and Bellolio were going to explain his absence when they arrived at the base. *Maybe my* commandante, *working with the captain of the* Piloto Pardo, *will send a launch back and search for me, assuming they can determine where we are. How could they* not *search for me?*

Now, however, survival was uppermost in his mind.

What are the orcas doing? Where are they? His body was shaking uncontrollably, as much from fear as from the temperature of the ice and the water penetrating his heavy clothes.

He again looked left and right.

Another minute passed.

Suddenly, out of the corner of his eye, he saw it . . . a wall of water, a 15-ton, 4-foot-high wall of seawater!

Rodríguez barely had time to comprehend what was happening when the wave hit, thrusting him and the dead seal into the air and down the backside of the ice into the water. Instantly he felt a sharp pain in his left chest, an excruciating pain that took his breath away. The numbing cold of the ice-laden water had stopped his heart. Before his hands could reach his chest, the jaws of a six-ton killer whale clamped down on his waist. The orca's three-inch-long teeth ripped through his clothes, the whale's jaws crushing his flesh and bones.

Shaking him violently, the killer dove instinctively for the depths with its prey, dragging Rodríguez's lifeless body down 200 feet to the bottom of the channel. Two other orcas took the seal, ripping it in half. Blood sprayed everywhere. The killing spree was over in less than ten seconds.

Except for seal blood on the ice and one of Rodríguez's gloves floating on the water, there were no signs of what had just happened. The orca pod disappeared into the ocean's depths. The only sounds were from sea water and small pieces of ice lapping against the side of the launch.

Lucero and Bellolio, hunched down in the launch, watched from a distance. They saw it all, every grizzly detail. Their faces were expressionless.

"Well, I guess we were warned just in time," said Lucero. "Rodríguez got greedy." He took off his left glove, removed his parka hood, and combed his hair back with his fingers. Then, after wiping his forehead with the back of his greasy parka sleeve, he put on his hood and glove, took a deep breath, shrugged, and said, matter of factly, "It wouldn't have worked out anyway."

Photo by Myrtle B. Cohen, the author's mother.

This story is an edited excerpt from the author's novel *Cold Blood: The Antarctic Murders Trilogy* (see Book I, *Frozen in Time: Murder at the Bottom of the World*). From December 1961 through early March 1962, Dr. Cohen participated in the XVI Chilean Expedition to the Antarctic. The US Board of Geographic Names in October, 1964, named the geographical feature Cohen Islands, located at 63° 18' S. latitude, 57° 53' W. longitude in the Cape Legoupil area, Antarctica, in his honor.

http://www.amazon.com/dp/B00O47W1PW

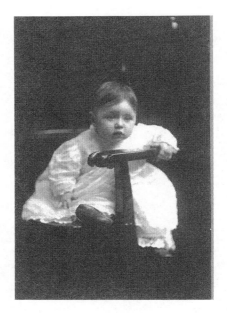

The author's mother, Myrtle (age one), who used to tell him stories of how *her* mother would scoop her up when a Gypsy caravan came to town, run into their house, lock the doors, and pull down the blinds.

The Reading

When it came to the occult, Leonie Mercier never was one to listen, not even to her *Defante Mère,* her poor sainted mother, Philomine. For as long as Leonie could remember, the woman, in her grave some four years now, had told Leonie fortune tellers were not to be trusted . . . which explains why Philomine always visited *two* tarot card readers—monthly—until a year before her death.

It wasn't that Philomine didn't believe what they foretold. She did. She admitted as much to Sophronia Beliveau, a Cajun friend who lived down the road in Palmetto, four miles west of the old concrete bridge over the Atchafalaya River. But her acceptance of the paranormal came with a proviso. "The important thing to keep in mind," she told Sophronia, "is that, life being what it is, 'tis better to get two opinions than be a *faut carot** caught in a glass jar. That way you have options!"

It was only a matter of time, of course, before the Fates exacted revenge on Philomine for attempting to thwart their will, an event that occurred almost a year prior to her death. At the time she had sought a tarot card reading from Madam Ophelia on the north side of Lebeau, just as she had done for as many years as she could remember. Distressed by what her other reader, Madam Roselle, had told her a day earlier about her beloved son, Otis—a big clumsy man everyone called *Grand Beedé*—she now sought a more encouraging view of Otis's future.

Alas, it was not to be. Madam Ophelia's reading was anything *but* encouraging. In fact, it was far worse than Madam Roselle's. So when the Louisiana State Police found Otis—who everyone agreed had been born under a bad sign—drowned in the bayou west of

---

* a big black grasshopper

27

Levee Road the next morning, *exactly* as had been foretold by Madam Ophelia, Philomine concluded knowing the future was not such a good thing. From that point forward she decided there would be no more visits to Madam Ophelia's *or* Madam Roselle's. No more tarot readings, period!

Leonie's curiosity was piqued. "Why did you stop having your fortune read?" she asked her mother several weeks after Otis's passing. Distraught over her son's death and guilt-ridden for not having warned him of the readings, especially the one performed by Madam Ophelia, Philomine explained to her daughter what had happened. Not only did she tell Leonie about the accuracy of Madam Ophelia's reading, but also warned her about the perils of knowing the future. Leonie dismissed the entire discussion with a wave of her hand. "I won't even listen to such foolishness," she said.

The guilt from having known her son's fate and not having intervened was more than Philomine could bear. Within a year she was dead. Some say she died of a broken heart. Abraham Duval, the tanned, leathered-faced Creole who cut her grass, said he knew she was going to die when he saw an alligator crawl under her house the day before her death.

Still, Leonie rejected the occult and things like alligators foretelling death. It was enough to tolerate her mother's dependence on tarot cards, palm readings, and crystal balls as well as the many superstitions foisted on her from the time she was little. From childhood on, for example, Leonie had been told Otis's mouth was crooked because he had slept with the Moon shining on his face.

To Leonie, anything derived from tarot cards and other such contrivances was as worthless as were the horoscopes found in her daily newspaper. Born under Leo, the fifth astrological sign of the zodiac, she'd laugh out loud over breakfast every morning after randomly selecting one sign upon another, reading the associated horoscope, and thinking about how it applied to her life. As far as she was concerned, the horoscope for a Scorpio, say, on any given day was as relevant to her life as was the horoscope provided under her own sign. "What a crock!" she would utter with distain.

Not that anyone heard her. Leonie's daughter, Ida, was away at college in Lafayette while her former husband, whom she had divorced five years earlier, probably was on some oil platform in the Gulf of Mexico. Or was it the Gulf of Oman? Alzophine Dufrene, who worked at Surette's meat market in Lebeau, mentioned overhearing someone say Leonie's former husband was working in the "Gulf," but exactly where she couldn't remember.

Leonie couldn't care less. Rémy had always been a *bon rien*—a good-for-nothing man. For as long as they were married—15 years to be exact—he'd rarely held any job longer than six months. He no longer was her problem. As far as she was concerned, it was good-bye and good riddance.

Someone who *was* her problem, however, was Ida. Willful even as a child, she became even more unmanageable when Leonie and Rémy divorced. Then age 13, Ida immediately started dating older boys. Problems with drinking and promiscuous sex soon followed, though somehow, Leonie was able to keep Ida in high school. However, the two women fought constantly. Rémy, of course, always took Ida's side, going so far as to send her money or whatever else she might want whenever Leonie cut off her allowance. One Saturday night in Ida's senior year, Leonie and Ida had such a knock-down, drag-out fight over car keys that Ida sent Leonie to the hospital with a horrific gash over her right eye. For her part, as a result of charges filed against her by Leonie, Ida spent the following week in juvenile detention.

Still, Leonie felt an obligation to see Ida through college. *Once she graduates, she's on her own,* she would tell herself. *At least I can say I did my best . . . I did what I had to do.*

With Ida an adult, at least in the eyes of the law, there was little Leonie could do to curb her daughter's self-destructive behavior. But as a mother, she worried. Greatly. She also was apprehensive, believing one night there'd be a rap at the front door, and the State Police would tell her something had happened to Ida. When that happened, what would they tell her? That she had been found raped and beaten, or that she had been involved in an automobile accident. Perhaps they'd say she was in the hospital, recovering from having overdosed on alcohol or drugs. Maybe, after identifying themselves, the priest accompanying the police would ask her to come down to the morgue in Lafayette and identify Ida's body.

The thought of her daughter's death didn't bother Leonie as much as she thought it should. In many ways, Ida was already "dead" to her. Certainly, she no longer felt any love for the child. Whatever love had existed died years ago, a casualty of the constant abuse and mental anguish Leonie had suffered at her daughter's hands.

In Leonie's mind, it was just a matter of time before the knock came. But when would it come? Sooner or later? The suspense was killing her, and in her mind, there was only one way to find out.

"So, you're *Defante* Philomine's daughter," said Madam Ophelia, shuffling the deck of 78 tarot cards—22 major arcana cards and 56 minor ones—over and over again as she hummed softly to herself. "I'm sorry about your brother. I know it came as a terrible shock to your mother."

She placed the tall deck in front of Leonie, who cut it in half. A grandfather clock in the corner behind the fortune teller chimed three times, marking the hour. Even with the curtains drawn, the afternoon sun made its presence felt, giving the room an eerie glow.

"So, my dear, you wish to know about your daughter, Ida," she said, confirming what Leonie had said when she called to make the appointment.

Leonie nodded. "Yes," she said in a barely audible whisper.

Reassembling the deck, Madam Ophelia dealt five cards face down on the table in the form of a horseshoe. She explained that from her vantage point, the five cards represented, in order from left to right, Ida's *Present Position, Present Desires, the Unexpected, the Immediate Future,* and *the Outcome.*

After pulling back the sleeves on her blouse, Madam Ophelia slowly turned over the first card representing Ida's *Present Position.* It was *The Fool.*

The fortune teller nodded. "I see an interesting young woman in front of me, one who acts with spontaneity and lives in the moment, a woman who does the unexpected and acts on impulse. She takes crazy chances, is always heading into the unknown. With her, anything goes. She feels carefree, uninhibited. The woman may be enjoying life at the moment, but she is taking a foolish path."

Leonie nodded but wondered. *Was this a lucky guess? Or did she base her comments on something she remembered my mother had said in one of her sessions?* There was no denying the fortune teller had described Ida to a T. But was this by chance, a mere flip of the coin, the draw of the cards? Leonie couldn't tell.

Madam Ophelia turned over the second card, which was intended to represent *Present Desires.* It was the *Eight of Wands.*

"Oh yes," Madam Ophelia proclaimed, "how fitting this card should follow *The Fool.* I see your daughter getting caught up in change, wanting to rush into something new, make a move, doing

30

something quickly. She wants to finish something up, end a chapter in her life, bring something to a conclusion."

I'm not surprised, thought Leonie. *The child is going to do something impulsive, and it will be the end of her.* She hung her head, turned, and stared at the floor to her left, focusing on nothing in particular.

Madam Ophelia cleared her throat. Leonie, startled, turned her attention back to the table, where the psychic revealed the third card, representing *the Unexpected*. It was *The Devil*.

"Oh my, this is very bad," Madam Ophelia intoned. "I foresee a bleak future for the woman . . . a cold, dark world. She will allow herself to be controlled and become addicted and enslaved. She will be surrounded by evil, caught up in unhealthy situations. Unfortunately, she will be ignorant of the truth and unable to sense the darkness that is about to descend upon her."

A shiver went up Leonie's spine. This sounded all too familiar, Ida being controlled by men who enslave her by plying her with liquor and perhaps drugs—evil men intent on dragging her down little by little until, like a frog being boiled in water, she no longer can resist.

Madam Ophelia reached for the fourth card, the one representing *the Immediate Future*. As she turned it over they saw the *Seven of Swords*. "Ah yes, the lone wolf, the one who is running away." The fortune teller nodded. "I expected it to appear, given what we already have seen. Your daughter will continue to run away from herself, from her demons, and take the easy way out while hiding the truth. She will hold you at arm's length for some perceived sin she believes *you* committed, deceiving herself while all the while punishing you. She will be content to maneuver behind the scenes, be two-faced, lie, and let you take the blame."

Leonie was startled. It never had dawned on her the root cause of her problem with Ida was the unresolved relationship between Ida and Rémy. It had begun with Leonie and Rémy's separation, their eventual divorce, and then, at least in Ida's mind, what she must have perceived as her father's abandonment of her. Leonie now realized Ida blamed *her* for the divorce and for the absence of Rémy in their lives. And periodic visits with Rémy had done nothing to quell Ida's hatred of her mother for the pain she was perceived to have caused. In fact, Ida's visits with Rémy only served to make matters worse. *How could I not have seen this?* Leonie asked

31

herself. *And even with this knowledge, what can I do? Rémy will undermine me at every turn. Hasn't he always taken her side, sent her money and whatever else she wanted?*

Madam Ophelia extended her hand to the fifth and final card, the one representing *the Outcome*. Slowly she turned the card on its back, revealing *Death* riding a pale horse and carrying a sickle.

Leonie put her hands to her mouth and gasped. Then, a strange calm overtook her as the sound of the fortune teller's voice receded slowly into the background. If Philomine's experience with Otis were any guide, there was no question now in her mind: her nightmare of uncertainty was almost over.

It wouldn't be long before she heard a knock at the door.

Photo by Dora Rubinstein, the author's grandmother.

For another story involving tarot card reading, read the author's Young Adult (YA) novel, *The Hypnotist*, which was written under the pen name "Alyssa Devine."

http://www.amazon.com/dp/B00V41FIG0

Professor Richard Conrad Emmons (1898-1993), a member of the University of Wisconsin-Madison Department of Geology faculty for 45 years. The only thing "Con" valued more than a good cup of coffee was a student's curiosity.

On Making Coffee and Other Scientific Endeavors

As usual, University of Wisconsin-Madison Professor Jonathan Conrad Fairclouth III was late for his 8 a.m. Monday morning class on Advanced Paleontology. In fact, his students, current and otherwise, could not remember his *ever* having arrived on time for *any* class, often stretching the obligatory 20-minute waiting period for a tenured professor to the very last second. Now, with a minute to go and the students in his Geology 205a lecture section beginning to pack their books and laptop computers, Fairclouth appeared, lecture notes grasped firmly in his left hand, a porcelain coffee mug emblazoned with Bucky Badger held tightly in his right.

To the professor, coffee was more than a morning staple. Brewing it was a ritual and the liquid itself—the "nectar of the gods," as Fairclouth called it—was something to be savored. So, as was his practice, the first order of business, the *very* first thing discussed at the beginning of every lecture, was that morning's brew and the precise process by which it had been prepared.

"I tried a new blend this morning," he intoned with a twinkle in his eyes. The students perked up. Some knew that look. They had seen it last semester when Fairclouth substituted crystals he had made using maple candy for one specimen on a mineral identification quiz.

"Kopi luwak coffee!" he blurted out. "That's the key!"

"Oh boy," Mary Wilson muttered under her breath, raising her eyebrows. A senior intent on pursuing a career in petroleum engineering, she gave everyone in the class a run for their money, both academically and physically. Smart, attractive, and a former star of Washington High School's track team in Milwaukee, she'd already been accepted for postgraduate work by the Colorado School of Mines, where she intended to pursue a doctorate.

"What?" asked Jarod Sanger, who was sitting to her right and still half-asleep after a weekend of barhopping on State Street.

Wilson leaned toward him, and covering her mouth with her right hand, whispered, "The coffee he's drinking . . . it's made from beans that have passed through the digestive systems of Asian palm civets. The stuff is unbelievably expensive."

Sanger made a face of a youngster who had just been given castor oil. "Are you f—?"

Wilson put her right forefinger on her classmate's lips, stopping not only his outburst but more importantly, the possibility Fairclouth might single them both out for special attention. Fortunately, the professor had moved on, and by the time the two turned their attention back to the podium, Fairclouth already was discussing the brewing process he had used that morning, including a review of his lab-quality borosilicate glass percolator, the water's characteristics—filtered, neither distilled nor softened—and the precise percolation time needed for the finely ground kopi luwak coffee. In addition, he reviewed how, precisely, he had ground the beans to the point where the coffee would pass through a #40 sieve. He left nothing out. Not one detail.

The students had heard much the same before. As a captive audience, however, they could do nothing but sit in silence while the "master" waxed poetic on the joys of brewing this morning's cup o' joe.

It drove them crazy! It also chewed up the first 10 minutes of the class. And given the professor had arrived 20 minutes late, whatever he had to say now on the topic of advanced paleontology would have to be squeezed into the remaining 20 minutes of the 50-minute period.

Not that the professor cared. Learning the material wasn't *his* problem. He knew it. And the textbook he had selected, together with the supplemental notes he had distributed on the first day of class, were more than sufficient to give students the knowledge they needed to pass the quizzes and final exam from which their grades would be determined.

But this was only part of the story, only part of what made Professor Jonathan Conrad Fairclouth III "tick." What he valued most was a student's *curiosity*. Whom he sought out were those who thrived on acquiring knowledge—not because they were under some compulsion to learn but because they truly were inspired by something they had read, heard him say, or observed in class.

"Give me a curious student," he would say, "and I will give you a valued member of society." True to his word, some of today's leaders in academia—specifically in the fields of sedimentology, stratigraphy, stratigraphic paleontology, and X-ray crystallography, among other disciplines—and in industry—specifically in such commercial enterprises as geophysical exploration, mining, and oil and gas extraction—earned their master's and doctoral degrees under his direction.

This is not to say the concept of time, in and of itself, was not important to Professor Fairclouth. The subjects of his innumerable studies, experiments, scientific papers, and lectures spanned hundreds of millions of years of geologic time. In particular, he devoted a good portion of his life to the study of curled-shelled creatures known as ammonites, which lived from the Devonian Period to the Cretaceous Period (roughly from between 420 million and 65 million years ago). Perhaps because of this enormous expanse of time, something few can even wrap their heads around, you got the feeling a few minutes here or there were of no importance whatsoever to the professor. And you'd be correct. If he didn't finish a lecture today, there'd always be another in two or three days. "What's the rush?" he'd ask if someone attempted to move things along. "Everything in due time."

According to some of his colleagues, Fairclouth would have been just as happy if time stood still. It was true. In many ways the man was an anachronism, from the way he dressed—he delivered his lectures at this time of year in a tweed suit, starched white shirt, and bow tie—to what he drove: a white, 1983, meticulously maintained Chrysler New Yorker with 14,000 miles on the odometer. The actual mileage was 114,000, but the mechanism on the console displayed only the last five digits.

This penchant for taking a *laissez-faire* attitude towards time was such that he maintained what many considered the old-fashioned concept of an "open door" policy toward visitors, one in which a student—any student, whether his or not—was welcome to drop in at any time and discuss anything with the professor, no matter the subject, no matter the time required. Unlike many of his colleagues, Fairclouth wasn't one to hide in the field or lab or to

37

shirk his classroom responsibilities by declining to teach certain courses because, selfishly, he wanted to pursue his research. To him, teaching was, first and foremost, a responsibility to be taken seriously. More to the point, to him it was a sacred responsibility.

So, having missed a few classes in which the professor discussed the ammonites of the Devonian Period—those that lived more than 400 million years ago—I trundled off one early October afternoon to the Lewis Weeks Hall for Geological Sciences, intending to engage the good professor in a discussion about the creatures.

I found him hunched behind his massive weather-beaten walnut desk in a corner office not more than 12 feet square, an office covered from floor to ceiling with bookshelves that overflowed with, and sagged under the weight of, a ton of scientific and scholarly journals, periodicals, and publications from all over the world. An old pendulum schoolhouse clock kept time on the wall next to the office's only window, which, though somewhat grimy, framed a courtyard looking splendid in its full fall regalia.

The room's atmosphere was quite agreeable. A large glass ashtray on the left side of the desk held two pipes. In it, ashes still smoldered with the faint scent of the aromatic blend of tobaccos the professor smoked. Below the ashtray was a stack of scientific reprints, each endorsed, I'm sure, with the obligatory "With the compliments of the author" scribbled in the upper-right-hand corner. A rolled-up copy of Madison's *The Capital Times* had been unceremoniously dumped into the wastepaper basket. God forbid he used the same container for the contents of his ashtray, something I'm sure must have concerned both the department staff and the building custodians.

Behind him, on the credenza, were various scientific awards and research instruments. "Never buy what you can make," he would tell his lab students, pointing with pride at the various devices he had designed and fabricated, some with the help of master machinists in the university's machine shop. A prolific author, he was always in the process of penning—and I do mean *penning*, with ink pen and paper—one scientific paper or another if not acting as a reviewer for major geological journals in the United States, Canada, and Europe.

And still, though you might think the pressures from his teaching and other obligations would have driven him into a frenzy, I found him to be the very picture of serenity. Perhaps it was the absence of a computer in his office, though there certainly was one on virtually everyone else's desk in the department. His desk phone—there was no cell phone in sight, nor had I ever seen him use one—was of simple construction, with three push-buttons on the console below the touch-tone keypad: two for incoming lines and one for call holding. For all intents and purposes, the office really had not changed—*had not evolved*—in form or function for decades. In it, time had stood still. To my eyes, it could just as easily have been a day in 1975 as it was now, in 1995.

He was oblivious to my presence, so I knocked softly on the door jamb.

Fairclouth's head jerked at the sound. Looking up, he recognized me instantly. "Come in, come in," he beckoned, setting down a paper he had been reviewing and putting his red pen aside. "How can I help you?"

I explained the purpose of my visit. He was delighted, ammonites being among his favorite topics.

"Of course. Let's chat." The professor opened the lower right-hand drawer of his desk and extracted a folder from which he withdrew a photograph of an ammonite from the Devonian Period. The coiled shell in the photograph—it looked a lot like the modern nautilus—had been carefully sliced open, revealing in plan view the creature's internal structure. It was partitioned into a collection of adjoining chambers, each separated by a wall which, in this case, was slightly curved.

"Isn't she a beauty? Lived in shallow marine waters, she did. See the simple suture pattern?" He pointed to the pattern that marked where the internal partitioning walls intersected the outer shell.

"You can't miss these suture marks, they're easily recognizable. In this case, of course, they're very simple . . . we're in the Devonian."

These creatures were a thing of beauty, all right. It was easy for me to understand why the professor was so taken with them.

"They make great index fossils, you know," he continued as he pulled another photograph from the folder. "They're found everywhere, you know, so they can be used for dating the rocks in which they're found."

He handed me the second photograph. *This is interesting,* I thought as I studied it. The crenulated and complex sutures I observed in the shell of the second ammonite stood in sharp contrast to the simple sutures of the first specimen. I almost did a double-take.

Fairclouth laughed. "Caught you by surprise, didn't it?"

"Well, I certainly wasn't expecting such a remarkable change."

"They did evolve rapidly, that's for sure," he said. "Makes them a great help in dating marine rocks. This one is from the Triassic Period—about 250 million years ago."

It was easy to understand the love he had for the field from the way he looked lovingly at the photographs and spoke of the creatures.

The old clock chimed once, but Professor Fairclouth evidenced no sign of having heard it. I knew we both had obligations: I, a 1 p.m. lecture in a course on Sedimentology and Stratigraphy on the building's 2nd floor; he, a two-hour lab on Tidal Sedimentation to be conducted in the building's basement. Neither of us rose.

"Now," he said, almost proudly, "look at this one."

The photograph he thrust into my hand was that of an ammonite from the Cretaceous Period. The label at the bottom clearly showed the creature was dated to 70 million years ago. The suture marks—that is, the marks where the internal partitioning walls intersected the outer shell—were highly crenulated and complex, full of all manner of twists and swirls.

Neither of us said anything for a minute. Finally, smiling wryly, he asked, "Do you think there might be more here than meets the eye?"

I hesitated. The professor was known to have a good heart. It wasn't his nature to draw a student into a trap, only to use a question such as this as a pretense to demonstrate his superior knowledge or embarrass the novice. "Well," I ventured timidly, "it took 330 million years, give or take, but it would appear that, as time progressed, things got more and more complex until, in the end, the organism became extinct."

"Bingo!" cried the professor. "So, why is everyone in such a hurry these days to speed things up, to add complexity to their lives when it all can come to no good end? Relax. Life is short. Enjoy what you have. Take time to 'be in the moment.' "

He looked at the clock on the wall. "I know, I know . . . you thought I'd forgotten about my next class, didn't you?" He chuckled. "Well, I still have a good 10 minutes before they pack up and leave." With that, he rose, grabbed some notes from his desk, and pushed his chair back.

"Don't you have somewhere to be?" he asked as he turned toward the door.

"Oh, I guess. But you know, I never was able to take your course in Tidal Sedimentation—I simply couldn't work it into my schedule. Do you mind if I sit in on today's lab session? Just out of curiosity, of course?"

Photo used by permission of the Department of Geoscience, University of Wisconsin-Madison. Appreciation is expressed to Emeritus Professor Robert H. Dott, Jr., PhD, Department of Geoscience, University of Wisconsin-Madison, for his assistance in obtaining this photo and for permission to use it here.

The pirate tipped his hat to Collette and was just about to pass them when he reached into his jacket, pulled out a pistol, and shot Matthew through the heart.

Encounter on All Hallows' Eve

Broadway, New York City, Halloween, October 31, 2010. The scene had all the appearance of Chalmun's Cantina located in the pirate city of Mos Eisley on the planet Tatooine in the *Star Wars* universe. While Jabba the Hutt as well as the Aqualish were absent from the Great White Way, there was no shortage of their earthly counterparts.

Among the more prevalent were prostitutes dressed as young girls; young girls dressed as prostitutes; "prostitots"—scantily dressed girls of age three and four with garish rouge, eyeliner, lipstick, and coiffured hair—escorted by their mothers, some of whom were dressed as cheerleaders; clowns; the usual smattering of political figures—costumes usually worn by boys; movie stars; cowboys; and in general, people dressed in just about every costume imaginable and some that left nothing to the imagination!

Tonight, this was the center of *our* universe. And as long as the crowd was peaceful, the police, who were in great abundance, tended to ignore those celebrants who were jaywalking and committing other minor illegalities. Room on the sidewalk was at a premium, and in places, progress was measured in baby steps as individuals inched their way toward whatever destinations they had in mind—if any.

It was into this maelstrom of humankind that international banker Matthew B. Richardson III and his wife, Collette, gently pushed their way out of the Lyceum Theater on West 45th Street following the opening night performance of the musical *The Scottsboro Boys*.

"*C'était magnifique*, Matthew." Collette grabbed his left arm and laid her head on his shoulder as they walked. "But this could

43

not be true, could it? Tell me this could not have happened in America."

"I'm afraid it's all too true, my dear. And this play only scratches the surface of one of the darkest periods in this country's history."

"But did you enjoy the performance, *mon amour*?"

"Actually, I did. But frankly, I'm concerned most people today really don't want to confront the ugly truths told in that story. If someone were to ask me, I think the show is a stunning theatrical success but will prove a box office failure."

They walked arm-in-arm toward Seventh Avenue, at which point they turned southwest and made their way toward Times Square. Ordinarily Matthew would have had his driver, Jafar, wait with his limousine in front of the theater. As the president, chief executive officer, and chairman of the board of Richardson Stanfield & Cooper, one of the largest investment banking and securities firms in the United States, he had a car and driver available to him 24 hours a day, anywhere in the world.

But tonight, in deference to his wife's pleadings to experience a Halloween celebration unlike any other in the country, or perhaps the world, he instructed his driver to wait for them on the northeast corner of Broadway and West 38th Street.

It was difficult for him to say "no" to her. Collette had entered his life in the spring of 2003, a time when he was experiencing deep anguish. A year earlier, Estelle, his wife of 30 years, passed away from ovarian cancer after a short but painful battle with the disease. In his mid-50s at the time and having no children, he faced the future with despair. "Hopeless" was the way he described it to his best friend, Sanjar Shahrestani, an Iranian-American who not only ran a large hedge fund but advised Matthew's firm on investments for its clients as well. The two men had known each other for 18 years. When Estelle was alive, the Richardsons and Shahrestanis could be found together on many weekends throughout the year, enjoying the opening of a new play on Broadway, dining in one of New York's finer restaurants, or simply relaxing by the pool at Shahrestani's magnificent home in the Hamptons.

After Estelle's death, Richardson threw himself into his work, sometimes arriving at his office in New York's Financial District by 5:30 in the morning and not leaving until well past 10 at night. His temper grew shorter with time, and even his executive staff, with whom he had worked closely for more than ten years, began calling him Ivan the Terrible behind his back.

Richardson's secretary, Grace Simons, a woman in her early 60s who had been with the firm since it was founded by Richardson's father almost four decades earlier, dissolved in tears one afternoon under a withering attack from her boss over having mislaid some dictated notes. By the time he cooled down and returned to apologize, the woman had cleaned out her desk and left the building, never to return. It was as if Matthew was permanently stuck in Elisabeth Kübler-Ross's second stage of grief—anger.

But all this changed in May 2003, when, on a business trip to Paris, he ran into Sanjar at a conference on international economic policy.

The two greeted each other warmly, throwing their arms around each other and patting one another on the back.

"Matthew, my dear friend, how *are* you? My God, it's good to see you." Of the two, Shahrestani clearly was the more enthusiastic.

"Sanjar, so nice to see you." Matthew managed a weak smile.

"Matthew, I've arranged for several clients to join me for a dinner cruise on the Seine tonight, and you'll join us, yes? I won't take "no" for an answer."

"Oh, Sanjar, as much as I appreciate your generous offer, I'm afraid I can't. I wouldn't make very good company."

"Matthew! I said I won't take "no" for an answer! Besides, I have a lovely young woman I want you to meet. Her name is—"

"Now wait a minute, Sanjar. I don't really think—"

"Matthew! This isn't about you. This is about a young woman who recently lost her husband. He was another dear friend and client of mine who tragically was killed in an automobile accident in the French Pyrenees last winter. His name was Rémy Marceaux and—"

"Not the young industrialist who had recently completed that €700 million acquisition of the shipyard in Saint-Nazaire? I read about his death. Tragic, simply tragic."

"It was a great loss . . . to his wife, to me personally, and, of course, to France. Madame Marceaux has been in mourning since his death, and I fear for her health. I want desperately to help her—and you as well. So put aside your feelings for a moment and consider this: if you would agree to dinner, I think I can convince her to join us by assuring her that the good company, fresh air, and fine food would be a tonic . . . and something good for her spirit, something her husband most assuredly would have wanted her to experience."

"I don't know, Sanjar—"

"Then it's done, my friend!" It was not easy to argue with his friend, regardless of the topic. "I'll make all the arrangements." He took out a business card and scribbled a location on the back.

"Give this to the taxi driver. The boat leaves Notre Dame exactly at twenty hundred hours. Don't be late! *Au revoir.*"

With that, he waved to an acquaintance across the auditorium's entrance hall and sprinted off, leaving Matthew looking down at the business card in his hand.

"*Au revoir*, Sanjar." His words were barely audible.

Richardson alighted from the taxi shortly before 8 p.m. and made his way down the stone embankment to the gangplank leading to the luxury dinner boat. He was greeted on deck by the captain and escorted inside by one of the ship's officers. His host already was aboard, standing next to the baby grand piano in the far corner of the ship's dining room, near the stern.

Sanjar waved him over. "Matthew. Matthew! Come here. I want you to meet Madame Collette Marceaux. Collette, *je voudrais présenter* Matthew B. Richardson III."

Collette, a woman of medium height whose short, blonde hair contained platinum highlights, was wearing a simple but elegant pleated, black cocktail dress. A perfectly matched string of 50 pearls hung around her neck. She was in her early 40s, yet looked as if she had just stepped off a runway show during Paris Fashion Week.

She looked up, smiled at Matthew, and extended her right hand, which he accepted and kissed.

"Charmed, Madame Marceaux."

"*Enchantée.*"

"I'm afraid my French is not good, Madame. I do hope we can work out a compromise of sorts, using English."

She laughed. "That is not much of a compromise, Monsieur. It will not be a problem." Her lilting French accent had a noticeable impact on him, and he looked smitten.

Sanjar smiled and quietly slipped away, leaving Matthew and Collette to get acquainted. Every once in a while he would glance their way, finding them first at the bar ordering drinks, then on the stern, pointing out and commenting to each other on the various landmarks, including a replica of *La Statue de la Liberté*, *La Tour Eiffel*, and *Le Grand Palais*, among others, as the boat made its way slowly up and down the river.

If Matthew had concerns regarding his ability to communicate with Collette, they were quickly dispelled. She was every bit as fluent in English as he was, having majored in the language at the *Université Paris-Sorbonne*.

Their conversation at dinner was animated, with neither spending much time talking to others at their table. The last anyone saw of them, around 11 p.m., after the boat docked and they had thanked their host and the captain for the evening, was when both got into the same taxi and were driven into the night.

After that, the two were inseparable. If Matthew was in Europe, whether in Paris, London, Berlin, The Hague, or Moscow, Collette would fly to his side. When he was in New York, she flew to be with him at least twice a month, staying in the Ty Warner Penthouse in the Four Seasons Hotel at $30,000 a night.

Within six months, they were married. Their lavish wedding was attended by 500 guests. Collette's younger sister, Adrienne, was her maid of honor. Sanjar served as Matthew's best man. The couple honeymooned for two weeks on a private island in the Indian Ocean before returning to New York City and settling into Matthew's two-story 8,600 square-foot penthouse apartment on Park Avenue.

Now, they were making their way, arm-in-arm, down Broadway, among the throng bent on celebrating the old pagan Festival of the Dead. Matthew was on Collette's right. Behind them, a man dressed as the pirate Blackbeard was gaining on them. He walked with an affected limp and had a fake parrot sewn on his left shoulder. No one paid much attention to him as he pushed his way through the crowd, bowing and smiling, the gold foil covering one front tooth shining in the bright light from the overhead street lamps.

As Blackbeard approached the couple from behind, he bumped into Matthew, startling him. "Sorry, Gov'nor."

The "pirate" tipped his hat, smiled at Collette, and limped on. When he was about 60 feet in front of them, he abruptly turned around and started limping toward them, bowing and smiling. Matthew and Collette immediately recognized him and started to laugh, seeing the fake parrot flopping back and forth on his shoulder. The pirate tipped his hat to Collette and was just about to

47

pass them when he reached into his jacket, pulled out a pistol, and shot Matthew through the heart. The sound of the discharge, already muffled, was further masked by the deafening cacophony emanating from the crowd, but there was no mistaking what had happened.

For an instant, Matthew froze. Then, he crumpled to the pavement. It took Collette a moment to realize what had happened. Then, she took one look at her husband and began screaming.

Dropping to the pavement, she pulled Matthew's head into her lap, smoothing his hair with her left hand and swaying back and forth, as if to soothe him. People were screaming, some out of fear, some for the police, who arrived quickly and cordoned off the area.

Within minutes, four ambulances and their crews were on the scene, tending to the wounded. But there was nothing they could do for Matthew.

And once again, Collette was a widow.

Photo: Shutterstock

This story is an excerpt from the author's award-winning mystery/thriller, *House of Cards: Dead Men Tell No Tales.*

http://www.amazon.com/dp/B005RIYQ7I

The novel also was cast into a screenplay, *Beware Those Closest,* an excerpt of which can be read on the author's Website:

http://www.theodore-cohen-novels.com/bewarethoseclosest-screenplay.html

"I rose ever so quietly, steadied myself on the pulpit in front of the large crucifix, and with Jesus Christ, Himself, looking down on me, took aim."

Unforgiven†

This wasn't his idea. There were plenty of other places where someone from Chicago on his first trip east could while away a Sunday afternoon in or around New York City. Broadway and Times Square came to mind. And Coney Island, too. But Peter had promised his dad when the man was on his deathbed two months earlier that he'd do it—something his father had never gotten around to doing and then couldn't because of his failing health: reconnect with his World War II platoon sergeant, Sergeant First Class (ret.) Davin Cassidy, 3rd Battalion, 505th Parachute Infantry Regiment, 82nd Airborne Division.

It took the help of a private investigator, but Peter, grown and in his mid-60s, finally had located the man at an assisted living facility near Palisades, New Jersey. Now, as he drove there from La Guardia on a sweltering Saturday afternoon in August, 2010, his only thoughts were to pay his respects, say what he had to say— "Just tell him what an honor it was to serve under him," were his father's last words—and be on his way. Mission accomplished, as it were.

He shook his head and wondered why he was even making the trip, finally laying the "blame," if that were the right word, on a son's duty to his father. It certainly wasn't out of love. Anything in the way of a relationship between Peter and his father had evaporated long ago when his father, ever distant and cold, shut him and his family out of his life for reasons Peter never could comprehend.

The assisted living facility, not as decoratively uninspiring as that of a hospital, was typical for its genre. It featured bright fluorescent lights embedded in sound-dampening ceiling panels, beige-painted walls on which were hung sparsely spaced, large but surely inexpensive reproductions of paintings by well-known

---

† "Unforgiven" won Honorable Mention in *Glimmer Train* magazine's September, 2015, Family Matters competition.

landscape artists, and a type of sanitary flooring used in such buildings, polished to a high gloss. The faint scent of a sanitizer used to control odors was unmistakable. An elevator, one of four, waited for him in the area beyond the dining hall and to the left of the glassed-in entrance to the new health and fitness center. Encouraged by the center's resident trainer, a lone senior could be seen struggling with weights on a pulley, barely raising them an inch or two from the stack before yielding to gravity and collapsing for a rest. Life's a bitch, thought Peter, as he stepped over the threshold and punched the appropriate floor button.

On the 6th floor, where the receptionist had directed him, everything changed. The floors were carpeted, with wainscoting the entire length of the hallway. Above the paneling, wallpaper rendered in a tasteful floral pattern lent a serene atmosphere to the space while flush-mounted fixtures provided more than sufficient light to assure the safety of residents and visitors alike. If he hadn't known where he was, he could have mistaken this part of the building for that found in most any hotel or motel. Architecturally nondescript, but generally not off-putting.

He had no trouble finding Davin Cassidy's room—number 637, to be exact—near the end of the hallway on the morning side of the building. The unmistakable voices of James Cagney and Jean Harlow could be heard through the door. There was no missing the Purple Heart decoration and small American flag tacked next to the door, just above the small brass plate on which the name "Cassidy" had been engraved. Whoever's behind that door, thought Peter, has been through Hell. He, of course, had no idea how bad it had been, given his father never would talk about "The War." That was a subject Peter and others in the family were strictly forbidden to discuss with the family patriarch, much less even raise in conversation.

Not that Peter hadn't tried. Once, as a freshman in high school, during a lull in conversation at the dinner table, he attempted to engage his father in a discussion of the Allied Forces' landings on Normandy, something that had come up in his history class that day. Before he could even finish a sentence, he was sent to his room in tears and told to never again raise that or any other subject pertaining to World War II in the house.

Lesson learned. The tension and embarrassment he felt that night welled up again in his mind, and he felt a knot in his stomach as he lifted his hand and knocked hesitantly on the door.

A thin voice beckoned. "Come in, it's unlocked." Inside he found a man in his mid-80s sitting in a large leather-covered recliner to the left of a sliding glass door that led to a balcony overlooking the Hudson River. The old man let his *Times* slide to the floor. Then he picked up the remote, switched off the television set, and adjusting his glasses, squinted at Peter for a few seconds. Finally, he spoke. "Do I know you, sir?"

"No, Sergeant Cassidy, we've never met. My name's Peter Donato. I'm from Chicago."

"Donato?" The old man cocked his head, his eyes looking up into his mind's eye. Clearly he was searching for something, *anything* that would trigger when or where he had heard that name before. And then the light of recognition dawned upon his face.

"I knew a Donato once. Antonio Donato. Yes! Corporal Antonio Donato. But we called him Tony. He was one of my squad leaders! Good soldier. Served under me in Europe. Are you related to him?"

"He was my father, Sergeant."

Cassidy squinted again, attempting to get a better look at the man standing before him. "Of course. Come in, come in." He pointed at a kitchen chair and beckoned Peter to bring it forward and sit. The old man smiled. "I shoulda known. You look just like I remember your father."

"That's not the first time I've been told that," Peter said matter-of-factly, sitting.

"Your father was a good man, son. The finest! We had a lot in common, you know," he said, leaning forward, "both coming from large families and all, and then, joining the Army to do our duty." Like Peter's father, Cassidy had lied his way into the Army on his 17th birthday and served three years, parachuting into France on D-Day and fighting right up until the end of the European Campaign.

"He often said the same about you, Sergeant." Peter was lying, of course. His father had never spoken of Cassidy—not once. But what could he say under the circumstances? "And on his deathbed—"

The color suddenly drained from Cassidy's face and his voice went flat. "Tony's dead?"

"Yes, sadly. He died in June. Pneumonia, the doctors said." Seeing the despair in Cassidy's eyes, and remembering why he had made the journey east, Peter quickly turned the conversation to its intended purpose. "But he made me promise I'd find you and tell you what an honor it was for him to have served under you." Cassidy, his lips pursed, wrung his hands but said nothing.

The silence made Peter nervous. "He also wanted me to tell you how much your friendship meant to him, something for which he was forever grateful." Peter watched as Cassidy nodded ever so slightly, but still the old man said nothing. If Cassidy had been listening to what Peter had been telling him up to now, it was difficult to say where his mind had gone, for his eyes, focused straight ahead, were looking right through Peter.

The silence was deafening, and Peter felt the knot in his stomach tighten. "He also wanted me to tell you how grateful he was for your having saved his men's lives at Sainte-Mère-Église." This was true, something Peter had learned from his mother when he was very young. Looking back, he would be hard pressed to say how this fact suddenly sprang to mind. But there it was, the words leaping from his lips before he even knew they were there.

The sergeant's eyes moistened. Not wanting to embarrass him, Peter looked away, toward the old weathered bookcase across the room. On its top shelf stood several framed pictures, including a color photograph taken of Cassidy and a family of four—two adults and, Peter assumed, their children. Maybe one of the adults is Cassidy's child, he thought. But where was Cassidy's wife? Best not to ask. Peter shifted his gaze right. The next picture, smaller and rendered in black and white, was faded, with yellowing around the edges. Pictured were four soldiers standing in front of a burned-out church. He recognized one of the men—a teenager, really—as his father; another, on the end to the right, almost certainly must be Cassidy, he thought. God, they were young. They should have been working at filling stations or doing the things kids 18 years old did at that time. Was the world totally crazy then? The four were smiling, flashing the "Victory" sign with the fingers of their right hands, their left hands firmly grasping the slings of their rifles, which were slung over their shoulders. Two had cigarettes dangling from their lips. Peter rose, walked to the book case, reached for the picture frame, and, returning to his chair in front of the sergeant, handed the photograph to the man. "When was this taken, Sarge?"

Cassidy regarded it for a moment and shook his head as if he could not believe how many years had passed. Then, as the

54

memories of what had happened in the days leading up to the moment captured in that photograph flooded into his mind, he slowly began to speak. "This was taken several days after we liberated the little French town of Sainte-Mère-Église following the invasion of Normandy. There were mines and booby-traps everywhere. It took a while until we were even able to bring in the people we needed to clean it up. But eventually we got the job done, gave the town back to its people, and moved farther inland."

Cassidy gently, almost reverently, wiped the dust from the frame with the fingers of his right hand. "Those were great guys, son. See the fellow on the left?" He poked a finger on the glass. "That's Stanley Cohn, a wise-cracking Jewish kid from the Bronx. Boy, no matter how bad things got, he could always make us laugh. Kept us in stitches, all right, especially when he spoke with a Yiddish accent. Next to him is your dad, who was Roman Catholic, of course. He and I always attended Sunday Mass together. To his left is Walt Sutton. He was a devout Baptist from Dallas. And that's me on the other end, an old Irish Catholic from Boston. Rank didn't matter. Neither did religion or background. We were like brothers. We were never out of each other's sight."

He paused and slumped in his chair, the picture frame falling to his lap. "Stanley was killed two days after this picture was taken when we were ambushed just to the south, in Carentan. Walt died in the Battle of the Bulge. The medics tried to save him, but his wounds were massive. Your father, who thought he should have provided better cover for Walt as they were moving up on a machine gun nest, held him in his arms when he passed. It was just before Christmas, 1944. At Bastogne. We were attached, then, to the 101st Airborne Division. The worst fighting I ever saw." Cassidy shook his head as if even now he still could not believe it. "And to think Walt almost made it through the war.

"Your father never was the same after that. It was like the light went out of his eyes . . . ." His voice trailed off and his focus drained.

The room again fell silent. Now it all made sense . . . the long periods of silence at the dinner table, the total and absolute prohibition against discussing anything related to World War II, the vacant look he often saw in his father's eyes when he chanced to look over at him while the family was watching television together. Now Peter understood, or at least he *thought* he understood, the pain his father must have endured all those years—his demons in

55

the night—and his total inability to talk about The War, much less tell anyone how he felt. A feeling of guilt overwhelmed him, and he felt sick to his stomach. If only his father had been able to talk about it . . . to someone, *to anyone.*

Stunned, Peter rose almost without thinking, and taking the picture with his left hand, shook Cassidy's hand. "Thank you for your service, sir." Cassidy looked up slowly, hardly appearing to hear what Peter had said. His mind was elsewhere, thousands of miles away on a battlefield that had long ago fallen silent in honor of the dead. So while Sergeant First Class (ret.) Davin Cassidy, 3rd Battalion, 505th Parachute Infantry Regiment, 82nd Airborne Division, gathered his thoughts and again paid his respects to the fallen of World War II, Peter turned with a tear in his eye, took a few steps, and returned the picture of the four infantrymen to its place of honor on the bookshelf.

When he turned around, he was surprised to see Cassidy struggling to his feet with the help of his cane. "Wait here, son. I wanna show you something." The sergeant walked with difficulty, and perhaps some pain, into his bedroom, which was off to the left of the small hallway at the entrance to the apartment. In a few seconds Peter heard a dresser drawer being opened and the sound of the old man rummaging through its contents. Soon he returned. In his left hand were an oval aluminum dog tag and its chain, which he handed to his visitor. A name and military unit had been punched in German into the tag. The most remarkable feature of the piece, however, was the bullet hole in its center. Peter wondered what the story behind it was as he ran his fingers over the ragged edges on the back. As he looked closer, he saw the unmistakable signs of faint, reddish-brown blood stains.

Cassidy slowly lowered himself into his chair and set his cane on the floor. "Remember the church in the picture, son?"

Peter nodded. "Well, our unit had been pinned down for more than a day by a German sniper in the bell tower. Trouble was, we couldn't get a tank or other piece of artillery in there to take him out. From the sound of it, we thought the guy was using a Karabiner 98k." Cassidy shook his head. "He was taking a terrible toll on our guys. We lost half your dad's squad just getting into position in front of the church." At this point Cassidy leaned forward and started to whisper, as if he were briefing Peter on a Top Secret mission. He also started embellishing his delivery with hand gestures, painting a picture of the action as he relived that day more than 65 years earlier in Sainte-Mère-Église.

"So, after dark, I worked my way 'round to the back of the building and into the sanctuary, where I crouched behind the pulpit. 'Long about two in the morning, I heard the bastard making his way slowly down from the bell tower—I dunno why he was comin' down—maybe he needed to grab more ammo or take a leak. I couldn't see nothin', bein' it was pitch black and all, but I heard him. He was taking very slow steps, feeling his way down, real careful-like. My heart was pounding so hard I thought it was going to jump out of my chest. All at once I see the flare from a match he struck on the stone wall of the spiral staircase. He musta thought he had gotten down far enough from the top so no one would see the light from a match."

Peter almost stopped breathing as he listened to the old man's story, so intent was he to hear every word.

The sergeant continued. "Anyway, he soon appeared and stopped at the bottom of the stairs. I rose ever so quietly, steadied myself on the pulpit in front of the large crucifix, and with Jesus Christ, Himself, looking down on me, took aim. Then, just as the match began to flicker, I held my breath and slowly squeezed the trigger. I guess his dog tag must've been right in front of his heart because the bullet went straight into his chest, and he dropped without uttering a sound. And that was the end of him."

Peter said nothing, but nodded ever so slightly. He gave the appearance of understanding what he had just heard but in truth, he didn't. He couldn't. He couldn't even imagine what it must have been like to fight in World War II, much less how it must have felt to kill another human being.

The old man sat back, thought for a few seconds, took a deep breath, and shook his head. "What I did was a sin, you know. A terrible sin."

"What's that, sir?"

"Killing him in God's house of worship. I desecrated the sanctuary." Cassidy made the sign of the cross. "But he would've done the same to me, given the chance. In a heartbeat! And I had my men to think of, Peter—your father and the others. I had to look out for them. They were my responsibility, you know. Some things you do just because you have no choice!" He blurted the words out as if he were pleading his case before Jesus and God Almighty.

57

"Religion, morality, right and wrong . . . they had nothing to do with it. It was kill or be killed, as simple as that." Peter wasn't quite sure why he was telling him these things. Certainly, he hadn't questioned the old man's actions. "You do what you have to do to stay alive, son, and if you're lucky, afterwards, you try to make peace with God . . . that is, when the cries of the dying and the wounded no longer wake you from the nightmares that leave you soaked in your own sweat. But the fact is, I still hear their cries in the night, even after all these years. And after a while, I came to understand the price I'm paying for the sins I committed."

Peter turned and looked out the sliding glass door toward the Hudson River, as if he was checking the weather. As far as he was concerned, it wasn't his place to judge this man or what he had done. And nothing he could say or do could erase whatever guilt Sergeant Cassidy harbored, feelings that haunted him even after more than six decades had elapsed since he parachuted into Sainte-Mère-Église and took up the battle against the entrenched German Army.

After a few seconds, Peter stood, and placing the German dog tag and chain in front of the photograph of the "Band of Four," started for the door. But before he even could turn to say good-bye, he heard the sergeant speak. "I'm happy your father found peace, son."

It was impossible to miss the tinge of envy in the old man's voice.

Photo: Ruins of Martincourt sur Meuse church, France, May, 1940. Source: Wikimedia Commons. Photo used here under the GNU Free Documentation License, Version 1.2 or any later version published by the Free Software Foundation.

This story was inspired by, and adapted from, the author's award-winning mystery/thriller, *Eighth Circle: A Special Place in Hell.*

http://www.amazon.com/dp/B00PG5QM1K/

**"Rendezvous with the British Antarctic Royal Research
Ship *John Biscoe* in the waters north of Astrolabe Island in the
Bransfield Strait, 14 nautical miles northwest of Cape Ducorps,
Trinity Peninsula. A British work party found what they
believe to be personal property belonging to
Lieutenant Commander Cristian Barbudo."**

Commodore, XVII Chilean Expedition to the Antarctic,
aboard the *Piloto Pardo,*
in a radiogram to
Captain Roberto Muñoz,
aboard the *Lientur,*
February, 1963

One Man's Journey Home

In early February, 1963, the radio operator aboard the *Lientur* came to the bridge and handed Captain Roberto Muñoz a radiogram. It was from the commodore on the *Piloto Pardo*, ordering the captain to rendezvous with the British Antarctic Royal Research Ship *John Biscoe* in the waters north of Astrolabe Island in the Bransfield Strait, 14 nautical miles northwest of Cape Ducorps, Trinity Peninsula.

The radiogram also informed Muñoz that the men of the *John Biscoe* had earlier been sent to erect an emergency hut farther to the north, on the coast of the Antarctic Peninsula, and that, during the course of surveying the area, the British work party had found what was believed to be personal property belonging to Lieutenant Commander Cristian Barbudo. Recovered from a rock beach and a nearby ice cave were the commander's laminated Chilean Navy identification card, some plastic-covered family photographs such as might be found in a wallet, a piton, and a badly damaged 35mm single-lens reflex camera.

The captain of the *John Biscoe*, Master John Williams, thought the Chilean Navy might want to return these items to the commander's family.

Captain Muñoz was directed to make radio contact with the *John Biscoe* at the earliest possible time on a frequency of 4042 kHz and to take possession of Lieutenant Commander Barbudo's personal effects as soon as possible.

Muñoz was stunned. He stared at the radiogram for several seconds, looked up at the overhead, and then, reread the radiogram.

"Begging your pardon, sir, but are you all right?"

"Oh yes, Sparks. It's just that this message took me by surprise. Call the *RSS John Biscoe* on a frequency of 4042 kilohertz and

61

determine her position. I need that information as soon as you can give it to me."

"Aye aye, sir."

"Engine room, slow to half-speed."

"Aye aye, sir."

"Navigator, bring me the charts for the waters around Astrolabe Island in the Bransfield Strait, northwest of Cape Ducorps, Trinity Peninsula."

"Aye aye, sir."

"Sir—"

"Yes, Sparks."

"Sir, the *John Biscoe* is standing off Astrolabe Island, coordinates 63°19′ South Latitude, 58°41′ West Longitude."

"Thank you, Sparks. Navigator, give me a course to Astrolabe Island from our current position."

"New course, one-two-seven degrees, sir."

"Helmsman, come right to new course one-two-seven."

"Aye aye, sir. Steady on course one-two-seven, sir."

Muñoz watched his ship come about. "Very well! Engine room, ahead full."

"Ahead full, aye aye, sir."

"Navigator, estimated time of arrival?"

"0300 hours local, sir."

"Sparks, call the *John Biscoe*. Convey my compliments to the captain, Master John Williams. Advise him that our estimated time of arrival is 0700 hours GMT. Advise him that we will maneuver in the waters off the island until 1100 hours GMT. Request permission to send a boarding party to his ship at 1300 hours GMT."

"Aye aye, sir.

"Commander De La Torre, you will accompany me aboard the *John Biscoe*. Dress whites for this occasion, Commander. We are going to pick up the personal effects of my good friend, Lieutenant Commander Cristian Barbudo. He fell into a crevasse last year while ashore with the geologic field party operating off the *Lientur*."

"I understand, sir. My condolences."

"Chief Petty Officer Acuña, you will be responsible for the launch. Dress whites as well."

"Aye aye, sir."

The radioman re-entered the bridge. "Sir—"

"Yes, Sparks."

"Sir, I have a message from Master John Williams. He sends his regards and will welcome your boarding party at 1300 hours GMT."

"Thank you, Sparks."

Captain Muñoz lifted his binoculars from his chest and scanned the horizon. The sea was covered with icebergs. *Some of those must be up to a quarter-mile across*, he thought, never failing to be awed by the majesty of Mother Nature and Her Antarctic domain. *With the wind and waters calm, the trip to Astrolabe Island should be uneventful. It's time to bring Cristian home.*

The *Lientur's* watch sighted Astrolabe Island at 0230 hours local time, and shortly thereafter, Muñoz made out the silhouette of the *John Biscoe*. She was a large ship, displacing some 1554 gross registered tonnage, and at 220 feet in length, was almost 80 feet longer than the *Lientur*. Her primary mission was as a British Antarctic Survey supply and research vessel. This included the responsibility of installing emergency huts on islands in the Bransfield Strait as well as at locations on the North Antarctic Peninsula.

Muñoz went to his cabin to rest for a few hours before showering, donning his dress whites, and having a small breakfast in his cabin with Commander De La Torre, the *Lientur's* executive officer, and Chief Petty Officer Acuña, during which he and Acuña briefed Commander De La Torre on how Lieutenant Commander Barbudo had lost his life the previous year.

"Recently," concluded the captain, "members of the British Antarctic Survey found some of Cristian's personal belongings among the rocks and in an ice cave near the shore. Master John Williams—" Muñoz paused, lowered his head, and turned to one side. Once he had regained his emotions, he continued.

"Master John Williams of the *John Biscoe* will turn Cristian's belongings over to me this morning in a short, formal ceremony aboard his vessel. It is my desire, with the commodore's permission, to return them to Señora Maria Barbudo and her children in Viña del Mar on my voyage back to Arica following the completion of this expedition."

The men nodded and finished their breakfast in silence. They could sense how traumatic Lieutenant Commander Barbudo's loss must have been for the captain, especially because he had been responsible for the safety and wellbeing of the geological survey party on which the commander lost his life. They certainly did not wish to add to his pain.

At exactly 1230 GMT—0830 local time—Chief Petty Officer Acuña ordered three seamen to place a motor launch in the water. Muñoz, Commander De La Torre, and he boarded the launch at 1250 GMT, whereupon its crew immediately set course for the *John Biscoe*. They docked at the larger ship's gangway exactly at 1300 GMT. Captain Muñoz was the first up the steps, followed by his executive officer, and then, by Acuña. Though the *John Biscoe* was a civilian ship, all three men were piped aboard as a courtesy. Muñoz and De La Torre saluted and shook hands with John Williams and his second-in-command, Mr. Bingham, whereupon the four men retired to the Master's cabin. Chief Petty Officer Acuña stayed on deck, at the top of the stairs.

"Welcome aboard the *John Biscoe*, Captain."

"It's a pleasure to be here, Captain. We sincerely appreciate your hospitality."

"May I offer you some tea or coffee . . . perhaps some biscuits or pastries?"

"Yes, coffee and biscuits would be nice, Captain."

"Steward, please."

"Yes, Captain."

"So, your message to the commodore said that you had found some of my friend's belongings."

The captain of the *John Biscoe* seemed surprised. "Lieutenant Commander Barbudo was your friend, Captain?"

"Oh, yes, Master Williams—"

"Please, call me John."

"Thank you, John. Please call me Roberto."

"Good! Roberto it is!"

"Yes, Cristian used to be my student in the naval intelligence course I taught at the Naval Academy. He excelled in the subject and later, went on to become one of the best investigators in our Office of Internal Affairs. We also became very close friends while he was at the Academy—so good, in fact, that he asked me to be the best man at his wedding. His widow, Maria, is a lovely woman. She has two beautiful daughters."

"Yes, we saw that in the photographs we recovered. Beautiful girls they are, too."

"If it isn't too painful, Roberto, may I inquire as to how he died?"

Captain Muñoz told the captain what had happened on the previous Chilean expedition, and why Cristian's body was never recovered.

"I'm so sorry, Roberto. That must have been very difficult for you."

Muñoz nodded. "Indeed it was, John. Never have I felt so powerless. There was nothing that I could do. But let me ask, if I may, how did your men come to find the things they discovered?"

"Well, as you know, Roberto, the UK, like many countries, deploys emergency huts in the Antarctic. These huts, bright red in color, dot both the coast and the interior of the continent. They are intended for use by injured or stranded explorers.

"We were erecting such a hut on the western shore of the Antarctic Peninsula close to where Lieutenant Commander Barbudo must have fallen into a crevasse. One of my men, walking along the shore, spotted a camera lodged among some rocks at the entrance to an ice cave, about 20 feet back from the shoreline. The ice cave had probably developed as a result of glacial melting and runoff. So, he and some others walked into the cave as far as they dared go. There, they found additional objects, which I also have for you today."

"I have to ask this, John. Did your men find Cristian's remains?"

"No, Roberto, regrettably not. Based on what they told me and my experience in this area, I'd say that there's an even chance his remains, if they came down with the melt water, were washed out to sea."

"I understand, John. Thank you. Please extend my grateful appreciation to your men for their efforts."

"I'll do that, Roberto. Thank you. They will appreciate those kind words."

Then, he took his napkin off his lap, folded it, pushed his chair back, and stood. Turning to the credenza behind him, he picked up a small, black, leather-covered box with the British Antarctic Survey emblem embossed in gold on the top. Returning to the table, he stopped where Muñoz was sitting. Captain Muñoz rose, as did Commander De La Torre and Mr. Bingham. Thus began the formal ceremony of returning Lieutenant Commander Barbudo's personal possessions to the Chilean Navy.

"Captain Muñoz, it is with great honor, and considerable sadness, that on behalf of Her Majesty Queen Elizabeth the Second and the British Antarctic Survey, I return to you the personal belongings of Chilean Navy Lieutenant Commander Cristian Barbudo."

"Master Williams, on behalf of the Chilean Navy and the Commodore of the Seventeenth Chilean Expedition to the Antarctic, I gratefully accept the return of Lieutenant Commander Cristian Barbudo's personal possessions."

Master Williams handed Captain Muñoz the leather-covered box, whereupon they exchanged salutes. Then, everyone sat again.

Muñoz opened the box. In it, on royal blue velvet with gold piping around the edge, were the personal belongings that had been recovered. Also included on official parchment was a statement addressed to the Admiral of the Chilean Navy, conveying to the Chilean Government the items found. The statement included the date, time, and location of the findings as well as a list of the items. It was signed by the Master of the *John Biscoe* on behalf of Her Majesty Queen Elizabeth the Second and the British Antarctic Survey.

Muñoz put the parchment back in the box and slowly closed the lid. He sat there for a moment, deep in thought.

It was Master Williams who broke the silence. "You know, Roberto, I think the worst thing that can happen to anyone is losing a friend and not having the opportunity to say goodbye. These islands and the shores of the Antarctic Peninsula, not to mention the Peninsula itself, are dotted with memorials to friends of mine, some of whom I had known for decades. They were good men, scientists and engineers, explorers and adventurers, all drawn to the Frozen Continent by the challenges it poses. Some came to work, others to escape something or someone in their former lives, perhaps a dead-end career or a failed romance, you name it.

"But here is one of the last places on Earth where men can test their mettle against Nature and show the world, if not themselves, what they are made of. Tragically, some never make it home. I remember Oliver Burd, Eric Platt, Ronald Napier, David Statham, Geoffrey Stride, Dennis Bell—who can forget 'Tink?' —and just last year, Roger Filer. Aye, good men, they were." He lowered his head.

"So, like you, Roberto, I have my memories of friends long gone. It's part of life, but an unfortunate part, to be sure. You're lucky, though. At least you can bring the commander's widow some consolation. Having that picture of his two daughters will, I'm sure, bring her great comfort."

The silence in the room was broken only by the sound of the ship's chronometer sounding the hour.

"Thank you, John. That was very kind of you. Even though this has been difficult, you and your crew have been of immense help.

"But I have taken up altogether too much of your time. I know you have a busy schedule. So, with your permission, Commander De La Torre and I will take our leave. However, if I may, John—"

"Yes, Roberto?"

"Would you please delay your departure for a few minutes after I return to the *Lientur?* It would give me great pleasure to send over a few cases of our finest Chilean wines for you and your crew to enjoy. Just don't tell my commodore where you got them. They are from his finest stock. CPO Acuña tells me there was an unfortunate mix-up on the dock in Punta Arenas during the loading of commodore's flagship, and the wine, which should have gone to the *Piloto Pardo,* somehow ended up on the *Lientur*." Muñoz winked.

The Master of the *John Biscoe* laughed. "Why, Roberto, that would be most kind of you. We'll be happy to stand by and pipe the cases aboard. And your secret is safe with me. We will gladly toast your health, the health of your crew, and the memory of Lieutenant Commander Cristian Barbudo at tonight's mess."

The men stood, and Muñoz tucked the leather-covered box under his arm. Then, returning to the deck, they all shook hands, whereupon Captain Muñoz and Commander De La Torre saluted the Master, turned, and descended to the waiting launch.

"Chief Petty Officer Acuña, when we get to the *Lientur,* stand by. I want to send something back to the Master of the *John Biscoe*."

"Aye aye, sir."

"You may take us to the *Lientur* now."

Photo: Antarctica, Big Stock Photo

This story is an edited excerpt from the author's novel *Cold Blood: The Antarctic Murders Trilogy* (see Book II, *Unfinished Business: Pursuit of an Antarctic Killer*). It was inspired, in part, by the death of ionospheric physicist Carl Disch, formerly of Monroe, WI (just south of Madison), who disappeared on May 8, 1965, while wintering over at Byrd Station during Operation Deep Freeze 65. (This was at a time when the author was completing his work leading to a doctorate in geophysics at the University of Wisconsin's Geophysical and Polar Research Center.) Officially, it was recorded that Disch became disoriented during a blizzard (the temperature was -45° F at the time), lost his sense of direction, and wandered away from the lifeline while transiting from Byrd Station Longwire to the Byrd Station main tunnel.

http://www.amazon.com/dp/B00O47W1PW

James Butler Hickok (May 27, 1837 – August 2, 1876)

On August 2, 1876, James Butler Hickok—known as "Wild Bill" Hickok—was playing five-card-draw poker at Nuttal & Mann's Saloon in Deadwood, Dakota Territory. Unbeknownst to him, Jack McCall entered the saloon and then, shot him in the back of his head, killing him instantly. At the time, Hickok held two pairs, black aces over black eights, known today as the "Dead Man's Hand."

The Dead Man's Hand

"I'd love to find a good poker game," said Martelli. The fact is, except for his family and the NYPD, poker *was* Detective Louis Martelli's life. Those trips he and his family took to Las Vegas every spring were taken in part so Martelli could spend several evenings playing five-card stud with some of the men with whom he had served in Kosovo, Kuwait, and Iraq. What was unusual about their sessions, however, was they all cheated, all the time. And they all knew it. The fun was in catching the other guys cheating. And when it came to cheating, Martelli was the master. Whether it was dealing from the bottom of the deck, card culling, card segregation, card assembly, or forcing errors of judgment by badgering his opponents, he was without peer. This is what made their Army reunions so much fun. Cheat, catch the other guys cheating, reminisce over old times, raise a bottle of beer to toast all who gave some in the war, and raise another bottle to toast those who gave all.‡

Special Agent Amanda Whitman, who ran the local undercover FBI office in Lancaster, Pennsylvania, didn't skip a beat. "Well, I've heard the people who own a roadhouse called Horsefeathers just south of Wrightsville on Route 624—that's on the other side of the Susquehanna River from Columbia—run an illegal poker game every night but Sunday in their back room."

Martelli was all ears. "What do you mean 'illegal poker game?'"

"Pennsylvania gaming laws as they apply to poker don't have any charges on the books for players, only for someone who is

---

‡ The phrase, "All gave some . . . Some gave all," was first stated in a poem by the same title published in 2003 by Don Tyson.
http://8thwood.com/all_gave_some.htm

operating a game for profit. So, the law will look the other way in cases where everyone in the game can be considered a player."

"Okay," said Martelli. "So, what's the deal with the people at Horsefeathers?"

"They charge $50 per person to get into the back room and then, when they close the game down at 11 p.m., they take 30 percent of the money on the table. If the state were to find out about this, the establishment not only could be charged under the Pennsylvania gambling laws but also, could lose its liquor license."

"Sounds like Martelli's kind of place," quipped Detective Sean O'Keeffe, Martelli's partner.

"Just be careful, guys. That place is frequented by an unusually rough crowd, and they don't play nice with strangers."

It was a little after 8 p.m. when Martelli pulled his and O'Keeffe's rental car into the gravel parking lot of Horsefeathers off Route 624 near Wrightstown. Being Monday, parking was not a problem, and he easily found a place near the front door among the few pickup trucks in front of the one-story building. Except for the neon beer signs, there was little to distinguish the building from many others they saw along the highway, housing companies that provided plumbing or electrical services, appliances, and the like.

The detectives, dressed in faded jeans, open shirts, old blazers, and loafers made their way into the roadhouse. Several patrons could be seen nursing beers along the length of the old wooden bar. The bartender, a gruff-looking man with a toothpick in his mouth, was busy rinsing glasses at the far end. Everyone looked toward the door when Martelli and O'Keeffe entered, but they quickly returned to their beers and conversations as the newcomers selected stools and sat.

The bartender dried his hands on the towel tucked into his belt, walked to them, and, setting coasters in front of them, asked, "What'll it be, gents?"

"Couple of Buds in the bottle," responded Martelli, flipping a $20 bill onto the bar.

The bartender reached into a cooler, withdrew two bottles of Bud, popped the caps, and set the frosty bottles on the counter. Then, he rang up the sale and gave Martelli $5 in change. Martelli pushed the $5 bill toward the bartender.

"Much obliged, sir," said the bartender, obviously pleased.

Martelli took a swig of his beer and, holding the bottle in his right hand, swung around backwards and, with both elbows resting on the bar, surveyed the room. "Well, I guess this is as good as it gets in these parts, Sean," he said softly, lest anyone hear them using their real names. They were, after all, working under cover with the FBI on a sting intended to bring down the mob, which was attempting to take over the trash and recycling business in Lancaster.

O'Keeffe looked over his shoulder. "If this is going to be our life for the next few weeks, just shoot me now. I had my fill of small towns when I was a kid."

That's Sean's anger talking, Martelli thought. *He didn't have the easiest childhood.* They had worked together three years before Martelli learned his partner grew up in the Midwest, Wisconsin to be exact. He was the son of a traveling salesman—farm machinery was his line—and a stay-at-home mom. His father was on the road three weeks out of four, and in his absence, O'Keeffe's mother took up with a steady stream of "visitors."

When O'Keeffe's father came home early one Friday afternoon and caught his wife in bed with another man, he threw her out of the house. Tragically, O'Keeffe's mother and her lover died a week later in a collision on a rain-slicked highway near Sun Prairie, Wisconsin. By that time, however, O'Keeffe had already been sent to live with his father's sister in Appleton, Wisconsin, where he stayed until he finished high school.

With money being tight, college was not an option, so O'Keeffe enlisted in the Army and fortuitously, found a "home" in the MPs. Following graduation from the US Army Military Police School at Fort Leonard Wood, Missouri, he did two tours in Iraq before returning stateside. After resuming civilian life, he put his military training to good use as a police officer in a small New England town. In addition, thanks to the GI Bill, he earned a bachelor's degree in law enforcement from the nearby state university. Following graduation, and upon meeting the NYPD's requirements for Detective-Specialist, O'Keeffe joined the New York Police Department.

"This is the America I never saw, Sean . . . the heartland. Maybe someday I'll drive the family through here to Gettysburg and beyond, maybe all the way to Yellowstone. Amazing what there is to see," said Martelli as he turned around and faced the bar.

He no sooner had finished saying that when the roadhouse door opened and two men walked in. One was tall—at least six foot and then some—and appeared to weigh 300 pounds or more. His head was clean-shaven and he walked with a distinct waddle, his arms swinging at his sides as he moved toward a door to the rear of the bar. Following him at a distance of some five feet was a thinner, shorter man with a blank look on his face.

Martelli and O'Keeffe glanced up briefly to look at them over their shoulders as they entered.

"Recognize anyone, Sean?" whispered Martelli, using his partner's real name.

"I do believe that's Tiny and his friend, Larry Halstead."

"You have a good memory. I think we have a score to settle with Tiny on Al's behalf, don't you?"

Both Martelli and O'Keeffe recalled what had happened earlier that day when they met Agent Al Knots upon their arrival at the FBI's undercover trash and recycling company office in Lancaster. The man, some six foot in height and weighing 210 pounds, was sporting a black left eye and a bandage covering eight stitches on his left cheek. Long story short, Matt "Tiny" Farmer, who was over six feet tall, weighed more than 300 pounds, looked like a gorilla, and picked up trash for the mob in Lancaster, did not take kindly to Knots and his partner, Agent Burt Linden, soliciting the mob's customers for the FBI's trash pickup company the previous Friday afternoon. So, after Tiny and his partner, Halstead, stopped Knots's and Linden's car on the street and Tiny forced Knots out of his car, the "Gorilla" sucker-punched the agent, sending him to the ER to have his face stitched together.

"Oh shit, Lou," said O'Keeffe, "our first day on the job and you're already going to beat the crap out of somebody?"

"Well, I hadn't thought about actually getting physical, especially with the Gorilla. I thought more in the way of beating him at poker."

Martelli and O'Keeffe watched as Tiny opened the door to the back room and both men marched in. Although their view was partially obscured by the pair, the detectives could see a poker table, chips, and two men already playing cards.

Let the games begin, thought Martelli. "Sean, give me all the cash you have."

Sean opened his wallet and gave Martelli $300 in $20 bills. Martelli took a similar number of $20 bills from his own wallet. Leaving a $20 bill on the bar, he rolled Sean's and his money into a bundle and bound it with the rubber band that had been securing his business cards. "Now, doesn't that make a pretty picture?" he said, setting the roll on the counter. Then he motioned to the bartender.

When the bartender was in front of them, Martelli picked up the $20 bill he had set aside and presented it to him. "My friend and I enjoy a good game of poker. We understand the house runs a *great* game."

The bartender looked first at the large roll of $20 bills sitting on the counter and then at the $20 bill being offered to him. He took the one from Martelli's hand, turned, and started for the door to the back room, saying, "I'll be right back."

The bartender returned in a few minutes. "You're invited to join the game in the back. It's private, and we want to keep it that way. It'll cost you $50 each to get in, and when I close it down at 11 p.m., the house takes 30 percent of whatever cash is on the table."

After giving the bartender their $100 "price of admission," Martelli and O'Keeffe walked over to the door to the back room, knocked, and waited. In a few seconds, Halstead opened the door a crack, peered out, looked them up and down, and then, opened the door for them to enter.

"Hi," said Martelli. "I'm Tony Mateo. This here's Shane O'Brien. We drifted into town over the weekend. Not sure how long we'll be staying but heard this was the place to find a good game of poker."

The three men sitting at the table appeared to have heard it all before and showed no emotion. "I'm called Tiny," said the Gorilla. "Larry's the one who let you in. These other two are Joe and Frank. We don't spend a lot of time on formalities, so have a seat and play."

Martelli sat to Tiny's right, with O'Keeffe to the right of Martelli. Halstead was on Tiny's left. *Tiny's even bigger up close,* thought Martelli as he shifted his chair slightly to the right, a consequence of Tiny's huge arm taking up more than its fair share of the space between them. *God, imagine having to sit next to him on an airplane.*

The men purchased their chips, drew cards to determine who would be the first to deal—Joe won the honor—and the initial game began. Joe called for Anaconda, and the game proceeded apace. *I'll*

75

just bide my time, thought Martelli, *and begin by helping Tiny build a nice nest egg. Then, as the evening wears on, I'll clean out Joe, Frank, and Halstead, and finally, I'll wipe out Tiny. O'Keeffe will figure it out pretty fast, and drop out at the appropriate time.*

The evening unfolded pretty much as Martelli planned. He was amused at the way Tiny attempted to cheat, watching him fat-finger the cards as he occasionally attempted to deal from the bottom of the deck. But by playing prudently, and manipulating the deck when he had the deal, Martelli saw to it that within 90 minutes Joe and Halstead were busted and O'Keeffe folded, saying, "This just isn't my night." This left Tiny, Frank, and Martelli playing, and Martelli had the deal. He called for five-card stud. Frank folded after the third card, leaving Tiny and Martelli.

Martelli had dealt Tiny the **Q♠** face down while giving himself the **10♥**. As the game progressed, Martelli dealt Tiny the **8♣**, **8♠**, and **A♣** while giving himself the **J♥**, **Q♥**, and **K♥**. Betting was brisk. In fact, both players were just about all in.

On the fifth "street," Martelli dealt Tiny the **A♠** and himself the **A♥**. At this, Tiny became angry. "Are you fucking kidding me? You dealt me the Dead Man's Hand!"

Indeed, Martelli had dealt him the poker hand comprising black aces and black eights, the hand named for the legendary five-card-draw hand held by Wild Bill Hickok when he was murdered by "Broken Nose Jack" McCall on August 2, 1876, in Saloon Number 10, Deadwood, Dakota Territory.

The Gorilla was beside himself. "You fucking cheated me," he said, spitting the words in Martelli's direction as the detective hauled in the night's total winnings, which, while uncounted, amounted to a little more than $1,500.

Suddenly, Tiny turned, sprung from his chair, and reaching under Martelli's left arm, lifted him out of his chair and held him in a hammerlock. Even though he struggled with all his might, Martelli was unable to touch his feet to the floor. As O'Keeffe rose to help his partner, Joe and Frank grabbed him and pulled him back from the table. Meanwhile, while Tiny pulled Martelli backwards, Halstead came around the table and took out and opened a switchblade knife.

This is not good, thought Martelli. He watched Halstead carefully as the man slowly approached him, flipping the knife back and forth from hand to hand.

And then, when Halstead was within two feet of Martelli, the detective, using his massive calf and thigh muscles, brought his left foot—the one to which his prosthesis device was fitted—up into Halstead's groin. For a split second Halstead appeared to recognize what had just happened, and then, the light in his eyes went out and he crumpled to the floor.

Tiny, surprised by the abrupt change in his partner's fortunes, momentarily released his grip, making it possible for Martelli, with his feet now firmly on the floor, first to bend forward and then to thrust his head back into Tiny's face with such force that it shattered the man's thin nasal bones. Crying out in pain, blood streaming from his nose, Tiny brought his hands to his face, releasing Martelli, who turned, grabbed the Gorilla's "family jewels," and squeezed so hard he thought the man's testicles were going to come off in his hand.

The rush of air into Tiny's lungs made a loud sucking sound. If there ever were anything that could be said to characterize extreme pain, this was it. Tiny's eyes bulged and the fingers of his hands, which he held in the air, were fluttering.

"Now, Tiny, would you be so kind and ask Joe and Frank to release my friend?"

Martelli gave another squeeze. Tiny gasped and wiggled his fingers.

"Joe, Frank, I think that's a signal to release my friend," said Martelli, without the least hint of emotion in his voice. "If I squeeze any harder, we'll be having Tiny's nuts for appetizers in a minute."

Joe and Frank released their hold on O'Keeffe, who went to the poker table and collected the cash. Martelli released his hold on Tiny, who fell to the floor and threw up.

After counting the cash, O'Keeffe left $450 on the table, pocketed the remainder, and headed for the door with Martelli. "By the way, guys," said Martelli as they were leaving, "here're our business cards. Give us a call if you ever want to play again."

"Do you think someone will say something about this, Lou?" O'Keeffe whispered.

"Are you kidding, Sean? What happens in Horsefeathers stays in Horsefeathers."

■ *Theodore Jerome Cohen*

Photo: Public Domain

This story was inspired by, and adapted from, the author's novel *Wheel of Fortune*. This novel is based on a sting conducted by a number of law enforcement agencies (including the FBI) some years ago in southeastern Pennsylvania that was intended to prevent the New York mob from taking over the trash hauling and recycling business in York, PA.

http://www.amazon.com/dp/B00TNEDSBC

"Oh, Daddy, she's six years old and so beautiful. You would love her. But she's always sullen and withdrawn. She never talks."

Tiffany Martelli to her father,
Detective Louis Martelli, NYPD

Violated

Something was wrong, of that he was sure. With two teenagers in the house, there should have been much more activity to greet his entrance—certainly, more in the way of commotion, or at least chatter and music—to greet his ears as he stepped across the threshold after a day in Manhattan. But there was nothing. Nothing but total silence, punctuated now and then by an occasional sound from the kitchen as his wife prepared the evening meal. And as much as he longed for a quiet evening at home, he found the silence eerily discomforting.

"What's going on, Steph? Where're the kids? Why's it so quiet?"

His wife, Stephanie, took his turkey dinner out of the oven and, after arranging the white meat, potatoes, and peas on a plate and adding cranberry sauce and a small salad, she set his dinner in front of him.

"Tiffany didn't have a good day, Lou. I've asked Rob to keep it down for a while so she can rest."

Martelli was alarmed. "Is she all right? Did something happen to her at school?"

"No. No, she's fine. But something must have happened at Mrs. Rodriguez's when she was over there after school, helping with her foster children. She came home shaking. When we hugged, she burst into tears. Oh, Lou, she just sobbed and sobbed. She almost couldn't catch her breath at times. I held her close, helped her climb the stairs, and got her into bed. It took a while, but I finally got her to fall asleep.

"I still don't know what the problem is. She kept saying she was all right, that there was nothing physically wrong with her, but she either wouldn't or couldn't tell me what happened."

Martelli scratched his head. From what Stephanie was saying, it appeared something traumatic had occurred. As to what it was, however, he didn't have a clue.

There were certain facts both he and his wife knew with certainty: twice a week after school Tiffany volunteered to help Mrs. Rodriguez, who lived several blocks from the Martellis' home, take care of her foster children. The middle-aged woman sorely needed Tiffany's assistance. Three weeks earlier the borough, tragically overwhelmed by hundreds of children in need of placement, had asked Mrs. Rodriguez to take on a third child—a six-year-old girl name Brianna. Mrs. Rodriguez accepted, placing an additional burden on the caregiver, who already was acting as the foster parent for twin four-year-old boys.

Tiffany always had come home from Mrs. Rodriguez's bursting with stories about how cute the children were and how much they loved her—and she, them. More often than not, her backpack was laden with drawings or artifacts the children had made for her using playdough or Popsicle sticks. Her room was full of these mementos. Some were gifts from earlier foster children who had either moved back with their mothers or on to other foster parents, while others were from the foster children currently residing with Mrs. Rodriguez.

Today, however, it appeared something had changed. Clearly, Tiffany's demeanor was unlike anything her mother had ever seen. And now, her father was upset as well.

Martelli, who had yet to take a bite, put down his fork, placed his napkin on the table, and standing, walked toward the stairs. "Maybe I should ask if she wants to talk to me," he said quietly to his wife.

Stephanie nodded as she took his dinner and prepared to keep it warm. "This may be one of those times when a daughter needs her father's shoulder," she said.

Martelli made his way slowly up the stairs and to his daughter's bedroom door, where he stood for a minute, listening. Not hearing anything, he knocked gently. A tiny voice responded from within.

"Who is it?"

"It's me, honey. May I come in?"

"If you want to," she responded, sounding tearful.

Martelli gently turned the doorknob and opened the door. The room was dark, with only the light from the hallway illuminating his daughter's bedroom. He saw her lying under the sheets, clutching her pillow. Even in the dim light he could see the puffiness around her eyes. When she saw him, she sat up, again burst into tears, and threw her arms up, waiting for him to hug her.

The big man quickly walked to her bed, sat down, and embraced his daughter, smoothing her hair and kissing her forehead. Neither said a word for a minute, though if one were to ask them later, they would say it seemed much longer.

Finally, Martelli spoke. "I don't know what happened this afternoon to upset you so, but anytime you want to talk about it, I'll be here to listen. No matter what it is, you know you can always talk to your mother and me. There's nothing—*nothing*—we can't talk about or work through together. We're family. Hell—and don't tell your mother I said that—"

Tiffany giggled. She knew if she did, her dad would have to "donate" $5 to the Swearing Jar, the mechanism by which the family raised funds to pay, in part, for their vacations.

"If you guys can put up with your mother and me, you can put up with just about anything," he said.

She giggled again. Taking a tissue from her nightstand, she dabbed her eyes and brightened some.

Martelli took her face gently in his hands, and looking into her eyes, smiled and asked, "So, do you want to talk, or would you rather rest a little more?"

"No, I think I want to talk," she said, tearing up, "but it won't be easy." She started to cry, then caught herself, nodded, and calmed down.

"Why don't you tell me what happened today, just as if you were talking to your best friend at school."

Tiffany nodded. "Well, after school let out, I went over to Mrs. Rodriguez's like I always do. The twins had colds, so she really had her hands full. She asked me if I would spend some time with Brianna. She's the new little girl the agency placed with Mrs. Rodriguez three weeks ago. Oh, Daddy, she's six years old and so beautiful. You would love her. But she's always sullen and withdrawn. She never talks."

"Never?"

"Never. I never once heard her say a word. Whenever I've gone to help Mrs. Rodriguez, I find her sitting on a small chair in the corner of the living room, watching TV."

83

"Okay, so what happened today?"

"Well, I came in and there she was. She was watching a movie about motorcycle gangs. I'm sure Mrs. Rodriguez would not have put that on for her, so I'm guessing Brianna must have been playing with the remote control.

"Anyway, as I came into the room, Brianna pointed to the TV and said, 'That's the man who hurt me.' I turned around to see this really mean-looking man with a mustache and ponytail who was wearing a bandana, leering from the screen."

"What did you do then?" Martelli asked.

"Well, I sat down in front of her and drew her into my lap. I asked, 'Are you sure? That's just a movie. It's not real, you know.' And she said, 'Oh, no, I'm sure. That's the man who hurt me . . . he always hurts me. And sometimes, when he's angry, he hurts my mother, too.' "

Martelli nodded. "I assume you changed the channel."

"Oh yes. In fact, I shut the set off and took her by the hand to the play table to make some things with playdough. It was the first time I was able to get her to do that. She even talked a little more, mostly about her mom and when she was going to see her again."

"Go on, Honey."

"Well, after Mrs. Rodriguez gave the boys some cold medicine and settled them down for a nap, she gave Brianna a snack. That's when I told her what had happened . . . you know, about the man on the TV screen and what Brianna had said.

"Mrs. Rodriguez pulled me to one corner of the kitchen and told me Brianna's mother's boyfriend had been molesting Brianna since the child was three years old. It was only by the grace of God that a neighbor had called police one night because of the noise in the mother's apartment. That's when Child Welfare Services was alerted to the abuse and took Brianna into their system.

"Oh, Daddy, how can *anyone* be so cruel to a child? What is wrong with this world?"

Martelli shook his head, reached out, and hugged his daughter tightly.

For the first time in a long time, he had no answers.

Photo: Big Stock Photo

This story was inspired by, and adapted from, the author's novel, *Night Shadows*. This award-winning novel addresses the subjects of child abuse, teen rape, teenage suicide . . . and revenge.

http://www.amazon.com/dp/B00J828Q20

Mulberry Bend
Little Italy, New York City, 1896

The Godfather

It was a few minutes before 9 p.m. when Detectives Louis Martelli and Sean O'Keeffe entered Luchini's on Little Italy's Mulberry Street. The area was a mere shadow of what it had been in 1910, and today, only a few Italian stores and restaurants could be found along the three blocks that 10,000 Italians once called home. Most of the restaurant's customers from the second sitting had departed, and except for an elderly couple in one corner and a few younger patrons nursing beers at the bar, the restaurant was deserted. Not that one expected anything different for a weekday night. Still, the lack of customers made the detectives uncomfortable, and they looked around the room and over their shoulders several times as if they were not sure what to expect. Finally, Martelli walked to the bar, motioned for the bartender, and asked for Don Bianchi.

"He's in da back, behind datt door." The bartender jerked his head toward a door at the back of the restaurant.

"Thanks. Come on, Sean." The men walked to the back of the restaurant. Martelli knocked on the door.

A thin raspy voice on the other side beckoned. "Come in."

Martelli opened the door and walked in, followed by O'Keeffe. The room was an anachronism, a throwback to the days some 70 years earlier immediately following World War II. Starkly furnished, it contained two well-worn brown leather couches, end tables on either side of the couches, one standing ashtray, an old oak office desk at which sat an elderly gentleman, and several hardwood chairs with armrests. A ficus plant (much in need of water) stood in one corner, its leaves bowed. Above it hung an ancient schoolhouse clock that long ago had ceased to herald the hours, its pendulum now and perhaps forever stilled by the passage of the very time it was intended to mark. Off in another corner stood three wooden filing cabinets, their yellowed drawer labels and broken handles giving every indication they, too, had seen their best years. Atop one cabinet was a pre-WWII FADA Model 115 "Bullet" radio, its ivory Catalin cabinet now turned dark butterscotch over the intervening years by the damaging rays of the sun. The room had only one window. It was unadorned save for the yellowed shade that had been pulled down to ensure the room's occupants some measure of privacy.

Two photographs had been hung on the wall behind the desk. The larger, measuring three feet wide by two feet high, was a photograph printed on matte paper showing a parade in Little Italy on VE Day, marking the end of WWII in Europe. Rendered in black and white, the photograph, like most of the people in it, had faded into history.

The second photograph was curious. Hung beneath faded, crossed Sicilian and US flags, it also had been printed in black and white on matte paper. Taken in the same room, it showed two men, arms around each other's shoulders, smiling for the photographer. From the calendar behind them, the photograph appeared to have been taken on a day in March, 1943. One of the men in the photograph bore a striking resemblance to the man seated at the desk. The other was the gangster Meyer Lansky.

In fact, the man pictured with Lansky was Don Bianchi's father, Tomasso. Lansky had come to Luchini's to meet with Tomasso and to ask if he would accompany him to the office of Commander Charles R. Haffenden of the U.S. Navy Office of Naval Intelligence, Third Naval District in New York, in order to discuss helping the US government. At the time, the Allies were preparing for the invasion of Sicily, and they were seeking as much information as possible, including maps, photographs, and other data regarding Sicilian facilities, roads, beaches, and the like, in preparation for the operation, *regardless of the source.*

Tomasso Bianchi was more than happy to assist his adopted country in providing extensive photographs and detailed descriptions of his hometown Licata, an important port city on the southern side of the island. As it turned out, it was the city taken by the 3rd Infantry Division of the US Seventh Army during Operation Husky—the Allied invasion of Sicily in the summer of 1943—the success of which was in no small way due to the efforts of the

Italian-American community in general and American mobsters (such as Lansky) in particular.

Martelli assumed Don Bianchi was the man seated behind the desk. He was nattily dressed in a black pinstripe suit, light blue shirt, and red and black stripped tie. A red silk handkerchief blossomed from his suit jacket's left front pocket. From all appearances—including his white hair and thick-lensed, horned-rimmed glasses—he was George Burns incarnate. A wisp of smoke curled upwards from the half-smoked cigar that lay in the dark brown glass ashtray before him. The cigar band read *Sigaro Toscano.* Two men in their 30s stood next to the Godfather, one to each side, their arms folded in front of them. They were dressed in dark blue, tailored Italian suits, white shirts, and solid-colored ties. Each appeared to be packing heat.

Don Bianchi spread his arms and smiled broadly. "Louis Martelli, welcome. You honor me with your presence. Would that your sainted father were with us for this occasion. And tell me, who is this young man you've brought with you?"

"This is my partner, Don Bianchi. It's my pleasure to present Detective Sean O'Keeffe."

"Welcome, Detective O'Keeffe. I am Don Alfredo Bianchi. We are pleased that you could join us this evening."

"The pleasure is mine, sir." O'Keeffe was not quite sure where all this was heading, but for now, he played the hand he was dealt.

"I'm afraid you have the advantage of me, Don Bianchi." Martelli chose his words carefully. "In truth, I can't recall my father ever speaking of you. Perhaps you knew each other when I was young, a time when memories tend to fade quickly."

"Indeed it was, my friend," Don Bianchi responded, "many, many years ago, not long after your father joined the Force. We had grown up together—"

Martelli had a look of surprise on his face.

"Yes, I see that surprises you, my friend. But it's true. And over the years, our paths took us in entirely different directions. He, of course, went into law enforcement. I, on the other hand, was . . ." Don Bianchi paused. He was searching for the exact phrase with which to describe his situation. "I was, shall we say, a victim of circumstances and ended up on the other side of society."

Martelli nodded and smiled. He understood completely and could empathize, given his own life's experiences and the people he knew from his childhood.

"But we always remained friends, Louis." He hesitated. "May I call you Louis?"

"Of course, Don Bianchi."

"And I never put your father in a position where his loyalty could be questioned or his integrity compromised . . . until that one night, oh so many years ago, when he found me bleeding to death in an alley not far from here, the victim of a gunshot wound to the stomach. Here, let me show you."

Bianchi opened his suit jacket and started to reach toward his belt, intending to pull up his shirt and show Martelli and O'Keeffe his scar. However, O'Keeffe, thinking the man was going for his gun, reacted instinctively by reaching for his weapon, which set off a chain reaction. Before Martelli knew what was happening, Bianchi's two bodyguards were reaching for their weapons as well.

"Whoa, whoa, guys!" Martelli cried, throwing his right arm across O'Keeffe's chest, freezing his partner's arms in place.

Bianchi started laughing.

"These young bloods, Louis. What are we going to do with them?"

"Ah, to be young again, Don Bianchi."

The Godfather picked up his cigar, which had gone out, pulled a butane torch lighter from his vest pocket, snapped the ignition button, and with the cigar held down at an angle to the flame, turned the cigar in his fingers while he inhaled using short puffs until the end glowed cherry red. Then he took the cigar out of his mouth, coughed—a deep, congested smoker's cough—and turning the cigar around, gently blew on the glowing end to ensure it had been evenly lit. Returning the lighter to his vest pocket, he sat back and blew a cloud of grayish smoke toward the ceiling.

Everyone relaxed, and the conversation continued.

"So, what happened that night, Don Bianchi? How were you shot?" Martelli asked.

"Suffice it to say, Louis, there had been a slight disagreement between two 'families.' "

"And what did my father do?"

"Well, if you can believe this, he stopped the bleeding with a pressure bandage he made from my shirt, commandeered a cab—

90

remember, he walked a beat—and drove me to a hospital. Once we got to the emergency room, he had me treated as the victim of an accidental shooting. He wrote out the report himself, stating I had accidentally shot myself in the stomach while cleaning my weapon. Then, he went back to the neighborhood, hunted down the guy who shot me, and after roughing him up a bit, warned him if he ever said another word about the shooting, he'd bring the full force of the law down on him and his 'family.' "

Martelli appeared surprised. "My father roughed the guy up? This doesn't sound like Pietro, Don Bianchi. I never saw him raise a hand to anyone."

"Louis, your father was many persons, some I'm sure you never knew."

The Godfather started laughing. "I remember when we were teenagers. Your father owned a 'lowered' 1940 Mercury 2-door sedan, black, with full skirts, duals, and a special aluminum flywheel. It could do 90 miles per hour in second gear and better than 100 in third. The car had a flathead V8 perfect for racing, no third shift being necessary. We spent many nights drag racing on Long Island's parkways. Your dad even learned to drive the car without lights. That trick and the all-black finish allowed him to 'disappear' more than once when the police were on our tail. Pietro used to do "rumrunners"—spins, you know—and pass a pursuing police cruiser going in the opposite direction, flat out. Then, he would cut the lights, and while the police struggled to turn around, he would slip the Mercury backwards into a stand of trees and bushes, there to watch as the police sped by, unable to see us."

"My father did that?" Martelli could not believe what he was hearing. To him, his father was a saint.

It was clear Don Bianchi relished telling this story. There was a twinkle in his eyes that had not been there before. "One day, the police came to your father's house and told Pietro's father—your sainted grandfather Claudio, God rest his soul—that they would be waiting for his son the next time he came to Long Island to drag race. Moreover, they said, if they caught him, it would be at least ten years before his son saw the outside of a prison. Well, that was the end of that. Your grandfather not only made your father sell the car, but he laid down the law. He forced your dad to finish high school, attend trade school, and eventually helped him qualify for the NYPD Police Academy."

91

Martelli shook his head in disbelief.

"Well, Don Bianchi," O'Keeffe exclaimed, "that certainly explains a lot about my partner."

Don Bianchi laughed and took a puff on his cigar. "Let's see, where was I?"

"In the hospital, sir," Martelli injected.

"Oh, yes. Anyway, I was released from the hospital three days later. Your dad and I never spoke about it again. There were no investigations or repercussions, the two 'families' kissed and made up, and your father and I went our separate ways, always careful to keep our distance." Bianchi put his cigar down, leaned forward, and folding his hands in front of him, looked Martelli directly in the eyes. "And I'll tell you something else, Louis. Lots of cops who walked beats in Little Italy took cash and other gifts from us in exchange for looking the other way. It was expected, and we paid them off. To us, it was a cost of doing business. But your dad, now there was a man of integrity. He never took a dime. Not one red cent. Never. Not that it wasn't offered to him. He always would say to my boys, 'You wanna give money away, give it to the orphanage at St. Mary's.' So, once or twice a year, in grateful appreciation for what your father had done for me that night, I would take tens of thousands of dollars in used $100 bills—real ones, not the counterfeit crap we used to pass in this town—stuff them in a big brown paper bag, and go to confession at the church adjoining the orphanage. The kids at the home never had it so good!"

The men laughed.

"Thank God for the sanctity of the confessional, Don Bianchi," Martelli exclaimed, shaking his head. "That's a terrific story. Did my dad ever find out?"

"No, I never told him, Louis. And I feel I still owe him a debt of gratitude. He saved my life that night. But he did more than that. The fact I lived is one thing. I shudder to think what might have happened, however, if your father hadn't stopped the war that had erupted between the two 'families.' So, in loving memory of Pietro, I'm going to do something for you. I have no particular knowledge regarding the circumstances surrounding the unfortunate event you're here about tonight, and frankly, I don't want to know what's going on. But word on the street is, the man who torched your wife's car last night and terrorized your family is Niccolo Prosperi. He can be found these days in the DUMBO neighborhood of Brooklyn. That should be enough information for you to nab him. And of course, I know I can count on you for the utmost discretion regarding your source."

Martelli and O'Keeffe rose. "Thank you, Don Bianchi. Thank you on behalf of my father, Pietro, my family, and the New York Police Department."

The detectives shook Don Bianchi's hand.

"Go in peace, Detectives."

This story was adapted from the author's award-winning mystery/thriller, *Eighth Circle: A Special Place in Hell.*

http://www.amazon.com/dp/B00PG5QM1K/

■ *Theodore Jerome Cohen*

Theodore Jerome Cohen's first serious attempt to write a short story for publication was in 1962 while he was working in Antarctica. The story he penned—about a man killed by a pod of orcas—was lost during his return to the United States. It wasn't until 2009, when he resurrected the tale and incorporated it in his post-modern novel, *Frozen in Time, Murder at the Bottom of the World*, that the horror of the episode, which was based on a real encounter by three Chilean Army enlisted men with a pod of orcas, appeared in print. Time did not dim the horror of what happened at sea that day!

Now, this story and others—*unusual* stories about Ted's life as a violinist, about a woman who seeks the help of a fortune teller to divine the future of her daughter, and about a university professor obsessed with the making of coffee—are vividly brought to life in the eleven short stories found in this book. They betray a writer who has walked a road less traveled . . . indeed, a road few people ever will travel in their lifetimes, giving us fictionalized glimpses into the lives, *and in some cases the deaths*, of the men and women he met through stories inspired by real life events.

Theodore Jerome Cohen is an award-winning author who has published more than ten novels, all but one of them mystery/thrillers. He also writes Young Adult (YA) novels under the pen name "Alyssa Devine." During the course of his 45-year career he has worked as an engineer, scientist, CBS Radio Stations News Service (RSNS) commentator, investor, private investigator, and Antarctic explorer. What he's been able to do with his background is mix fiction with reality in ways that even his family and friends have been unable to unravel!

All of his novels are based on real events . . . some from his own life, some ripped from the headlines. Of his writing in *Death by Wall Street*, for example, Gary Sorkin of Pacific Book Review said: "Similar to the writing style of Michael Crichton and Tom Clancy, Ted Cohen adheres to short chapters laying out a mental storyboard in the reader's mind. He possesses a writing style ideal for screenplay adaptation with visuals that can make for a good movie. Why wait for Hollywood—*Death by Wall Street: Rampage of the Bulls* is currently playing in a theater near you, the theater of your mind."

For more information on Dr. Cohen and his novels, the interested reader is invited to view the book descriptions, photographs, poetry, and videos that can be found at <www.theodore-cohen-novels.com>. For information on his Young Adult novels, visit <www.alyssadevinenovels.com>.

Made in the USA
Charleston, SC
23 January 2016